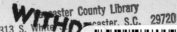
## The test

Stefan's face was nearly as white as his hair. His eyes by contrast were the purply-blue of blueberry Popsicles. Carolina wondered why he had the old-fashioned kind of wheelchair, the kind you pushed yourself, but she didn't think she should ask about that.

"What's the bird's name?" he asked.

"He doesn't have a real name. I call him Crow."

"Hey, do you think I could hold him?"

"I don't know," said Carolina. "He won't let my mom."

"Let me try," he said. "Please."

Carolina knelt so that Stefan and Crow were at eye level. Stefan put out his hand, palm down. Crow stomped his feet nervously. He turned to look at Carolina, glanced back at Stefan, stomped his feet some more. Then, to Carolina's surprise, he hopped onto Stefan's hand.

"It's an unusual story, with interesting characters and a strong plot, and it's fair to say that Crow steals the show, teaching Carolina how to accept change and to fly in spite of it."

—*Kirkus Reviews*

# OTHER PUFFIN BOOKS YOU MAY ENJOY

# Carolina Crow Girl

## VALERIE HOBBS

PUFFIN BOOKS

Carolina came about only because these terrific people cared about her
as much as I did: Barbara Markowitz, my smart and feisty agent; Frances
Foster, my wise and wonderful editor, and her right-hand gal, Elizabeth
Mikesell; Jack Hobbs, Judy Kirsch, Grace Rachow, James Coffee,
Mashey Bernstein, Dean Pananides, and Myrna Fleishman

PUFFIN BOOKS
Published by the Penguin Group
Penguin Putnam Books for Young Readers,
345 Hudson Street, New York, New York 10014, U.S.A.
Penguin Books Ltd, 27 Wrights Lane, London W8 5TZ, England
Penguin Books Australia Ltd, Ringwood, Victoria, Australia
Penguin Books Canada Ltd, 10 Alcorn Avenue, Toronto, Ontario, Canada M4V 3B2
Penguin Books (N.Z.) Ltd, 182-190 Wairau Road, Auckland 10, New Zealand

Penguin Books Ltd, Registered Offices: Harmondsworth, Middlesex, England

First published in the United States of America by Farrar, Straus and Giroux, 1999
Published by Puffin Books,
a division of Penguin Putnam Books for Young Readers, 2000

1  3  5  7  9  10  8  6  4  2

LIBRARY OF CONGRESS CATALOGING-IN-PUBLICATION DATA
Hobbs, Valerie.
Carolina Crow Girl / Valerie Hobbs.
p.  cm.
Summary: After eleven-year-old Carolina begins to make decisions for herself and no
longer feels constrained by her mother, she is able to let her pet crow fly free.
ISBN 0-14-130976-8 (pbk.)
[1. Freedom—Fiction.  2. Identity—Fiction.  3. Mothers and daughters—Fiction.
4. Crows—Fiction.]  I. Title.
PZ7.H65237 Car 2000  [Fic]—dc21  00-029087

Printed in the United States of America

*For Alise*

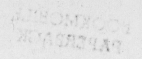

# 1

The wind called Carolina from sleep. Or a voice in the wind. Or a cry. She lay very still and listened. Overhead, through the mud-smeared windows of the bus, she could see a zillion stars. Black, black sky and stars too many to count. She held her breath and listened harder.

Earlier she had heard that same sound, but no one else had—a high, shrill cry. A scary sound, but sad, too. And then she knew just where it came from. She crept into her clothes, stepped carefully over the sleeping Melanie and down the steps of the old yellow school bus.

In both hands she carried Red's heavy flashlight. Red was Trinity's daddy, not hers, but the flashlight gave her courage just the same. Now that they had found a place for the bus, Carolina knew that Melanie would begin her search for Red. If they found him, Melanie said, they had found a home, here in California, where oranges came on trees and everybody surfed, even the dogs.

Carolina followed the path of Red's flashlight across the field, under the dome of black sky and stars. Dry weeds tickled her bare legs until she got to the place where the weeds stopped growing, where the ground was littered with eucalyptus bark and seedpods that smelled like cough medicine. Carolina liked the sound the bark made under her flip-flops. The sharp snap said she was coming, that whoever was out there had better watch out. But when she heard the screeching cry again, closer this time, her heart thunked hard in her chest as if she was really afraid.

Ahead was the cliff, and below it the ocean. Carolina pointed her light at the trees that formed a line along the cliff. They were very tall and shaggy and their branches drooped like the weary arms of soldiers at the end of a long march. "Come ahead," they said, or seemed to say. She stepped into their darkness, her light a yellow circle on torn, shaggy bark. Below the cliff, waves shushed in and out over the sand. Out on the dark water, the lights of far-away boats winked in the night like cat's eyes.

The cries came from a place where three great trees stood in a thoughtful sort of circle. Carolina went among the trees until she came to the last three. Then she stopped and beamed her light upward, into the dark caves of leaves. She had seen the crows who lived in these trees, who made their nests high, too high to see, then swooped suddenly down like packs of noisy black angels.

Inside the circle of trees the night held its breath. Carolina could hear the sounds of her own quick breathing and, high above her head, the leaves that whispered softly to each other. She beamed her light up the ragged bark of the tallest tree straight to the top, then down again to her own feet, which looked very small in their dusty blue flip-flops.

Then her light found something strange. A whitish lump, wet and soft-looking. She stepped closer, leaned over to get a better look, when, suddenly, up from the lump popped a screaming red mouth. She leaped back and nearly ran to the school bus, to safety, but she knew what it was, the screaming thing, and that there was no reason to be afraid. "Hey," she said softly, her flashlight shaking just a little in her hand. "Hey, bird."

Up came the head again. It was attached to the scrawniest chicken neck Carolina had ever seen. Except that it wasn't a chicken and it didn't seem to have a real head, just a folded-back beak and a hollow red cave for a mouth. Out of the mouth came angry desperate squawks that echoed over and over within the circle of trees.

"Hey, bird," she said, and the baby crow stopped screeching long enough to turn a dark suspicious eye. Carolina had never seen anything as ugly as this bird. It had no feathers, not a single one. Its skin was pinkish-white and pimply.

She beamed her light back up into the trees, into the dark spiny leaves where the nests were, where the bird's mother might be watching. Hunching down to make herself small in the dark, Carolina switched off her light, wrapped her arms around her knees, and waited. Darkness closed around her like a cupped hand. The baby bird gave a single pitiful squawk. There were other sounds, too, from things that sounded like the crickets she remembered from the South when she was small, things that scurried and clicked in the dry leaves. But no sounds from above, except for the whispering leaves, no flutter of great wings.

She tried to think about other things while she waited for the mother bird to save her baby. There was lots to think about, to wonder about. Somewhere, here or wherever Melanie took them next, Carolina would start sixth grade. She would be the new girl once again, made to stand in front of the room to introduce herself and tell about her family. She used to hate that more than anything. But then she learned to make a game of it. This time, she decided, her father would be an astronaut who got lost somewhere in space. If you looked in just the right place, she'd tell the class, if you looked at the exact right time and if the sky was dark enough, you could still see the trail of his ship.

She would not tell them that she lived with her single mother and baby sister in an old yellow school bus, not ever if she could help it.

Carolina waited for the mother bird until her legs were pins and needles, until the baby crow, exhausted, could barely squawk. Finally, she stood and clicked on her light. That was when the fat little lump threw all the life it had left into a final effort, one last screech, its whole body thrust forward at the light. Then it collapsed back into itself, its eyes pinched closed like an old sick person in sleep.

Carolina knelt and made a deep bowl with the front of her sweatshirt. She lifted the crow. Like Jell-O, it spilled all over her hand. Its scrawny legs fell on either side in strange bent angles.

Warm lump swinging in the bowl of her shirt, Carolina ran back to the bus, which was carefully hidden within a stand of thick bushes. Prying open the door, breathless, she dropped to her knees by the side of Melanie's mattress. "Melanie," she urged, nudging her mother's shoulder, "wake up."

Melanie rose on her elbows, blinking herself awake, her mouth thick with sleep. "What's up, sweetpea?"

"Look what I found," Carolina said. She opened up her sweatshirt and out came the crow. Its featherless wings flopped as it rolled onto Melanie's mattress.

"Oh my Lord, it's a bird!" Melanie pushed back her matted curls. She reached out her hand. The crow's head popped up, wobbled a little, and the mouth began to shriek. "Caro, where in the world . . . ?" Melanie frowned at her eleven-year-old daughter, whom she'd always counted on to make sensible decisions. "Where did it come from? Did it fall from the nest?"

Trinity woke up crying. Melanie crooned in her Southern drawl, "It's all right, darlin'. Caro's found a baby bird, see? Oooh, it's loud, isn't it?" And then she told Carolina to fetch some bread and milk. "The poor thing's starvin' to death," she said. Carolina rummaged through the food box and found a can of milk. She poured some into a cup and took it to Melanie along with what was left of the bread.

Melanie rolled a piece of the bread into a ball and soaked it in milk. Then she held the wet ball over the crow's head. Its black eyes opened. Its wobbly head shot up. But before it could squawk, Melanie dropped the bread in. It gagged and swallowed and then shrieked for more.

"There's something wrong with his legs," said Carolina, frowning. "He can't stand up."

"It takes a while," Melanie assured her. "There's probably nothing wrong. We'll let it spend the night, but in the morning, first thing, you take this bird right back where you found it."

Carolina dangled a milky ball over the baby bird's head. "But the mother won't come. I waited the longest time. I think she forgot about it."

"Of course she didn't forget, silly," Melanie said. "Mothers don't forget their babies."

Up came the crow's head; in went the food. "Never?"

"Never ever." Melanie tucked Trinity's blanket around her shoulders. "First thing in the morning, Caro, the bird goes back."

Carolina took the crow, the bread, and the milk to the back of the bus to her "room," where she had drawn a chalk line all around her mattress. No one was allowed inside that line without permission, not even Melanie. The bird began shrieking the minute she put it down. "Shush, bird," Carolina said, and as long as she fed it, the bird was quiet. She fed it until her arm fell asleep and her hand was wet and sticky with milk. She fed it until her eyes could no longer stay open. And when she fell asleep, her hand kept right on feeding it.

**2**

Stefan watched the girl from the window of his room, without moving so much as a hair, without blinking. She was about his age, he guessed, but smaller, a small quick girl with tanned arms and legs whom he might not have seen at all had the sun not been following her through the trees, pointing her out, lighting up her tangled golden-brown hair.

She looked wild to Stefan. She moved with the same cautious wariness of the animals that lived on his father's land, the ones whose movements he studied through his binoculars. In her arms she carried something, a basket or a bowl. He nearly reached for his binoculars to see what it was, but worried that she might look up and see him then, staring down from the window of his room like a spy.

He wondered what she could be doing on the Crouch estate. She had to have come from the other side of the trees, near the road, but not from the town. The land that had long been in his father's family was private. Everybody knew that. Just as they knew Stefan's father. His mother, too, of course. Their money had built an art museum and funded the physical-therapy wing at the hospital. One of the buildings at Stefan's school, to his everlasting embarrassment, was named for his grandfather, and thus for him. The Stefan Millington Crouch Gymnasium.

Stefan Millington Crouch III thought to himself, sitting at his second-story east-wing window, that no one would dare to trespass on this land if they knew how famous the Crouches were.

He watched the girl stop, tilt her head, and look up into the trees. Shielding her eyes from the bright sun, she turned slowly in a circle. When her back was to Stefan, he grabbed his binoculars. Adjusting the powerful lens, he brought her into focus. Blue rubber sandals, red shorts, white T-shirt with a torn sleeve. There was a Band-Aid on one of her stubby brown fingers. But what made his breath catch suddenly was the bird. Inside a basket within the girl's arms was a baby crow. Stefan, who knew more about the stretch of wild land along the cliff than any of the gardeners, and certainly more than his father would ever know, could tell at once that it was a recently hatched crow, *Corvus brachyrhynchos,* which had fallen from a nest.

Nature had taught Stefan a great many useful things. One of those things was patience, another was to trust his

11

intuition. He knew that the girl would not harm the bird. He watched her kneel and place the basket on the ground, her hair falling forward, covering her brown knees. When she stood and looked up into the trees again, he made a quick search of the grounds. If the girl wasn't careful, a stray cat would grab the bird, and that would be the end of it.

But nothing happened. The sun shone down, the girl stood among the eucalyptus trees, the crow squawked over and over again, the *car car* sound that young crows make, shooting its long neck straight up from its featherless body, but the mother bird never came. It happened that way sometimes, and Stefan knew that there was nothing, really, you could do to make it right. Except, of course, become its caretaker yourself. When the girl scooped up the basket and went off in the direction she came, Stefan had quite contradictory feelings. Though he had rescued many a bird on that land, he had never been so fortunate as to find a baby *Corvus brachyrhynchos*. The bird was his, or so he told himself. His father certainly would have said so.

But he could not fault the girl. She had attempted to re-unite the bird with its mother, just as he'd have done. She would have wanted to keep it as her own from the moment she found it, he knew that, because that would have been his wish, too. But she did the right, the proper, thing. She tried to return it to nature. He thought that they must be alike, this girl and he. Oh, not in any of the obvious ways. She wasn't in a wheelchair, for one thing. And she was, after all, a girl. But she seemed to have a reverence for nature like few children he knew. Few adults, for that matter. When she left his trees, she seemed to take all the light with her. He did his nature watching from then on with a new purpose. He watched for the girl with the bird. The crow girl, he called her.

**3**

Carolina had to admit that Melanie was right. There was nothing wrong with the crow. The more it ate, the stronger it became. In just a few weeks pinfeathers sprouted from soft pink skin, sprouts became sleek black feathers, and then one day, reaching for a bit of hamburger, the young bird stood straight up on its yellow stick legs. It seemed as surprised as Carolina. Still, it never left its basket, one bright eye or the other trained on Carolina no matter what she did, as if it was trying very hard to understand something. A week later, it climbed up her arm, step by step, sideways, bobbing its head up and down, back and forth. When it came to her shoulder, it settled there. "Okay," it seemed to say, "what do we do next?"

Carolina thought about names to give the crow. Pets were supposed to have names. But a wild bird wasn't exactly a pet. She began to call it Crow, which wasn't exactly a name. When she walked in the fields, the black bird perched on her shoulder, Carolina knew that it belonged there, in the tall, shaggy soldier trees, with its mother. But it never flew off, never left her shoulder. She grew used to having a bird on her shoulder, as if it had always been there.

"That bird needs to fly," said Melanie. It was a warm windy afternoon and they had walked across the field to the cliff above the sea, Trinity riding in her pack on Melanie's back, Crow on Carolina's shoulder. From where they stood, the world stretched away forever, gray sky and green water. Carolina said nothing, but her mind danced with the idea of flying, about how it would feel. She ran the back of her hand under Crow's chest, which made him step daintily onto her hand. "Are you ready to fly, Crow?" she said into his glittering dark eyes. She lifted him high above her head, but he clung with his claws to her fingers.

"You have to make him do it," said Melanie. "Just like his mother would. Here, let me try." But when she reached for Crow, he leaped onto Carolina's shoulder and turned his head away.

"He'll fly when he's ready," said Carolina.

"But he won't, honey. He doesn't know he's supposed to fly."

"Fry!" cried Trinity from her backpack.

"That bird thinks this is all there is to life," Melanie said. "Riding around on somebody's shoulder. It isn't right, Carolina. He needs his freedom."

Part of Carolina wanted Crow to fly, part of her wanted

15

him to stay right where he was. Where he was safe. Where he was hers. But she knew Melanie was right. Birds were meant to fly. Crow didn't seem to care one way or the other. He would watch others like himself crossing the sky with deep dips of their strong wings, but as soon as they were out of sight, he seemed to forget what he had seen. His world was on the ground, where he scurried about in search of bugs or bits of colored glass, anything shiny that he could hoard away in some spot even Carolina couldn't find.

Below the cliff, waves broke the surface of the water in flashes of white foam. A pair of gulls passed overhead, their white wings bright against the overcast sky. Melanie studied her daughter and the young black bird. Hesitating only a little, she said, "It's a good day to fly, don't you think?"

The wind blew Carolina's hair across her face. She pushed it back, squinting up at her mother.

"Go ahead," urged Melanie. "Give him a toss."

"Out there?" Melanie couldn't mean what she said. "Over the cliff?"

"It's what his mom would do, honey. Go ahead, let him go. He'll fly. You'll see."

"Fry!" cried Trinity.

Carolina stepped back, as if she couldn't trust her own mother not to grab Crow, though she really knew better. For as long as Carolina could remember, Melanie had encouraged her to make her own decisions, especially the hard ones. "Sometimes you have the dumbest ideas," she said, turning her back on Melanie and stalking away, flip-flops stinging the soles of her feet. Crow bounced lightly on her shoulder.

Melanie didn't know anything. How could she be sure that Crow would fly? He'd fallen once. That was enough. Maybe there was something wrong with his wings. Humans couldn't know that. Melanie's ideas really stank sometimes. Crow would fly when he was ready.

She stopped to let Crow listen to the cawing up in the branches where he'd been born. He cocked his head, side-stepping to the edge of Carolina's shoulder, where he did a little experimental hop. Excitement rippled through his body. "Talk to them," she whispered, but Crow just cocked his head and stomped his feet.

She walked until she came to the mansion at the far end of the trees. It was a huge three-story house with windows that looked out to the sea, but because its shingles were the color of tree bark, you could pass right by without seeing it. From a tiny window at the very top, a person with binoculars had stared down at her the day she tried to return Crow to his mother. All she could see of his face were two round glassy circles, fixed and staring like the eyes of a giant insect. Frightened, she'd grabbed up Crow sooner than she wanted to and hurried back to the bus. Today the window was empty, the blinds drawn.

Just then, as she watched, a door on the first floor opened and down a ramp came an old man in a wheelchair. Stopping at the base of the ramp, he looked up at the overcast sky. That was when Carolina saw that it wasn't an old man at all but a young boy, a boy with white hair. Curious, she stepped out from behind the tree to get a better look. Up came the binoculars, and she was caught again. "Wait!" cried the boy in a high-pitched voice as Carolina turned away. He wheeled his chair to the edge of a brick patio. When she saw he could come no farther, Carolina took a few steps closer. With a bump over the edge of the bricks, the boy came rushing toward her, dry leaves crackling beneath the wheels of his chair. He stopped just short of Carolina and Crow, a stern expression on his face. "This is private land, you know." Then, as if the clouds had cleared to let the sun through, his face changed. "But it's all right. I won't tell my father. What does he care anyway? He's never around."

"Where does he go?" What a strange boy, she thought. He talked as if he already knew her.

The boy shrugged. "Madrid, Rome, Timbuktu. Who knows? What's your name?"

"Carolina. What's yours?"

"The short version or the long one?"

"The short one, I guess."

"Stefan," the boy said, extending his hand. Carolina took it, wincing as his hand gripped hers. "Sorry," he said. "Sometimes I just don't know my own strength!" But he didn't look at all sorry. Or very strong either. His face was nearly as white as his hair. His eyes by contrast were the purply-blue of blueberry Popsicles. Carolina wondered why he had the old-fashioned kind of wheelchair, the kind you pushed yourself. But she didn't think she should ask about that.

"What's the bird's name?"

"He doesn't have a real name. I call him Crow."

Stefan considered that for several seconds. "I wonder what animals call themselves. Did you ever wonder about that? Whether they have names for each other. Joey, Julie, Sammy. Hey, do you think I could hold him?"

"I don't know," said Carolina. "He won't let my mom."

"Let me try," he said. "Please."

Carolina knelt so that Stefan and Crow were at eye level. Stefan put out his hand, palm down. Crow stomped his feet nervously. He turned to look at Carolina, glanced back at Stefan, stomped his feet some more. Then, to Carolina's surprise, he hopped onto Stefan's hand. Stefan became perfectly still. "He's beautiful," he said softly. "I've *never* held a crow, not a live one, anyway."

Carolina was relieved when Crow dipped his tail and hopped back onto her shoulder. "Melanie says it's time for him to fly. She tried to get me to make him do it, but I wouldn't."

"Crows fly when they're ready," the boy said. "When their tails get long enough. He's almost ready."

"I *knew* it wasn't time."

"He's probably got a family waiting somewhere. You can let him go pretty soon."

But pretty soon wasn't yet. "I don't think he's got a mother," she said.

"But he's got aunts and uncles. Maybe older brothers and sisters. They'll take care of him."

"Are you sure?"

"Sure I'm sure," the boy said. "I read all about birds. Other animals, too."

"Well," Carolina said after a while. "Melanie's probably looking for me. We'd better go."

She took a step back, then another, but he came right after her. "Is that your sister? Melanie?" He wore a plaid scarf around his neck and navy-blue knit gloves. His jacket was zipped to his chin. Didn't he know it was summer?

"Huh? Oh no. She's my mom."

"Why do you call her by her first name?"

"I dunno, I just do."

"Well, that's cool," said Stefan.

"Yeah, I guess. Well, bye," she said.

"Hey, will you come back?" He inched his chair forward, as if he meant to follow her home. "We can play pool or something."

"Pool?"

"Yeah. Haven't you ever played pool? It's a neat game. I could teach you, if you want."

Carolina had thought he meant a swimming pool and was glad that she hadn't given herself away. "No."

"Well, I'll teach you, then," he said. "I'm an Olympic champion pool player. Special Olympics." His purply-blue eyes danced. "Nah, only kidding! Will you come over sometime?"

Carolina wasn't sure she wanted to be any nearer the mansion than she was at that moment, and certainly not inside it. But she didn't want to hurt the boy's feelings. "Sure," she said. "Sometime."

# 4

Carolina had finally learned to whistle. Crossing the field from Stefan's house, kicking at seedpods and whistling a tune Red had taught her, Carolina glanced up and saw the black-and-white police car. She took off at a run, Crow's wings lifting, and was out of breath by the time she got to the bus.

Two policemen stood at the open door. Melanie glowered at them from inside.

"I don't make the laws, ma'am," one of the policemen said. He looked too young to be a real policeman, but he wore a dark blue uniform and spoke in a deep, authoritative voice. The other, who was older, stood behind, arms crossed over his barrel chest. "You're on private property," the young one said. "You living in this bus, or what?" When he tried to poke his head inside, Melanie pushed past him, forcing him to take a step back.

"This is our *home*," Melanie said. Crossing her arms, she drew herself up to her full height, only six inches taller than Carolina.

The policeman gave the dented yellow school bus the once-over and shook his head. "Just you and the kid here?"

"And the baby."

Carolina took Melanie's hand, more for Melanie than for herself. She could feel her mother's small hand shaking inside her own.

"Well, you gotta move on," he said. "You can't live here. I'm surprised nobody turned you in, but you've got the bus pretty well hidden back here. If Child Protective Services finds out you're living in some field, you could lose these kids." Frowning, he scanned the thicket of oak trees that separated the field from the road. "Try the trailer park just outside town. Maybe they have room for . . . for a bus."

"But you have to pay," Melanie protested. "Two weeks in advance."

"Well, I can't help that."

Then the older policeman stepped up. He smiled sleepily, as if he'd just awakened from a nap. "Looks like you've done a nice job with this old bus," he said.

"We did all the work ourselves," said Melanie, with a squeeze of Carolina's hand. "Well, almost . . ." Carolina knew that Melanie was remembering when they had first met Red up North. How Red hauled all the seats out but one and bolted the table in. The bus felt more like a real house then. "Would you like to see it?"

"It would be a pleasure, ma'am," said the older policeman, extending his hand. "Sergeant Carney." The younger policeman frowned. He wrote something in a tiny notebook and tucked it in his pocket.

Melanie took Sergeant Carney through the bus. From outside, Carolina could see her mother pointing out the curtains she'd sewed by hand, the bright blue bedspreads on each of the mattresses, the ninety-seven (going on a hundred) books in a handmade bookcase along the wall, the elastic cord that kept the books from falling out when the bus went around corners.

The younger policeman waited impatiently. He unwrapped a stick of gum without offering one to Carolina and stuffed it in his mouth. He glanced at the ground and poked the toe of his shiny black shoe at something in the weeds. Crow watched intently, looking from the policeman's bright badge to his shiny toe and back again. It was easy to see what the younger policeman thought about people who lived in buses. His disapproval made Carolina angry. At him, but at Melanie, too.

They had been living with friends in North Carolina when they first found the old school bus. For months Melanie had been looking for an apartment in a safe neighborhood that she could afford. At last she had given up. Then, at a county schools auction, she had found the bus. With their last bit of savings she bought it and drove it home. Laughing, she'd grabbed Carolina's hand and danced with her around the bus. They were going to be free, she told Carolina. They were going to live just like Gypsies. Take off whenever they wanted, go wherever they wanted to go, see the whole country. No more living in neighborhoods where children weren't safe, where doors had to be locked in the daytime. No more sneaking away in the night because they couldn't pay the rent. No more staying with friends who didn't really want them. Like Gypsies, they would travel all summer, and when September came, they'd find the best schools and the greenest parks and live right near them. It was the perfect solution.

Carolina had seen her mother get this excited many times. Sometimes it wasn't good. A long, sad time would usually follow. But Carolina had fallen in love with the bus, too. It wasn't the home they'd dreamed of having one day, the one with the little white fence and bright blue door, but it was a place all their own, a safe place.

They'd traveled that first summer, just as Melanie promised, staying in campgrounds alongside big sleek campers, cooking over campfires, reading from their ninety-seven books. Melanie hadn't graduated from high school—her biggest mistake, she said—and read for hours each night to make up for lost time. By September they'd traveled all the way across the country and it was time to settle down for a while. They chose a small town in Northern California, not far from the ocean, and Melanie found a job that first day. In exchange for a place to park the bus and a small salary, she cleaned the rooms at the Seaview Motel.

Fourth grade had been easy, just like all the other grades before. Making friends was harder, but Carolina was good at that, too. Then one of the girls found out about the bus. For a couple of days Carolina was the center of attention. Her new friends seemed eager to know all about her life. They wanted to see her room, and so she took them to the bus. She showed them the bright blue spreads, the curtains, the stickers from all the states they'd been to that they'd pasted on the windows. Melanie served cookies and cranberry juice.

Afterward, the girls wanted to know the whereabouts of Carolina's father. She said he was in Tunisia, as faraway a place as she could think of. They asked where he worked, what he did, how many pairs of jeans she owned, and if she got an allowance. The next day they left her out of jump rope and didn't choose her for softball, and before long she was eating lunch at a long table in the cafeteria by herself. She began to resent Melanie. She began to hate the bus, the stupid bus. "I want a real house, Melanie," she said.

"Melanie? Since when have I stopped being your mom?"

But Carolina bit her lip instead of saying what she wanted to say: That a real mom wouldn't live in a school bus. Real moms lived in real houses. They were married to the fathers of their children. So she kept calling Melanie Melanie.

Red started coming around that first summer. He was big and loud and filled the bus just by being inside it. Melanie, starry-eyed, said they'd found their home at last. But she and Carolina still lived on the bus, and Red came and went. In June Carolina got a baby sister. Then Red announced that he was taking his fishing boat south and Melanie pulled out the road maps. They headed down the coast the day after Carolina finished fifth grade. "Isn't it great to be on the road again?" cried Melanie. "Isn't it great to be free?"

"Maybe we can find my dad," Carolina sometimes said, even though she knew what the response would be.

"Your daddy doesn't want to be found, sweetpea."

Pressed within the pages of *The Swiss Family Robinson* was a photograph of her father. He was leaning against an old truck, his arms crossed over his chest, squinting into the sunshine as the camera snapped his picture. He looked like a high-school boy, not a father, and that's just what he was. Sometimes Carolina missed him. Then she wondered how you could miss somebody you didn't even know.

The policemen left, the younger one warning Melanie again that she would have to find another place—another *city,* he said—to park *that* bus. He wouldn't report them to the Child Protective Services Agency. Not yet; but he couldn't guarantee that they wouldn't find out. Melanie went into one of her slumps. "I'll never find a job here," she said. "And who knows where Red is? One of the fishermen told me Red was here all right but that he's gone up to Alaska after salmon. I guess we should go up there . . ."

"*Melanie . . . !*" Carolina cried. "We just moved here!" When Melanie went into a slump, you never knew what she'd do. Sometimes she slept all day, or wept for hours, her curly head sunk into her crossed arms. Sometimes she'd go off on long, solitary walks, leaving Carolina to watch the baby. Then, for no reason at all, she'd be her other self, the one Carolina loved best. In her husky voice, just a little off tune, she'd sing their favorite on-the-road songs or tell Carolina stories about growing up "back South." She wasn't like other mothers then. She was better.

"Well, what can we do?" Melanie said now. "We can't stay here. You heard what that policeman said. What if the . . . that *agency* he said . . ."

"Child Protective Services," recited Carolina, having said the scary words a dozen times already in her mind.

"Yes, that one. What if they try to take you two away from me?"

"But what about Crow? He *has* to stay here!"

"He's a *bird,* Carolina! I'm talking about you, about my *children*!"

"Well, I'm not going anyplace," Carolina threatened. "Go to Alaska, I don't care. I'm staying here. With Crow. I don't care what you do!" Her head still ringing with angry words, she put the bird in his basket and took him to the back of the bus, inside the chalk circle where nobody could go, *especially* not Melanie.

Carolina hated to cry. It seemed like such a baby thing, yet how could she help it? Wriggling beneath her comforter, she sobbed quietly into her pillow, nose dribbling and soaking her pillowcase. Why couldn't they just live like other people? Why was Melanie so *weird*?

As she drifted off to sleep, Carolina thought about the boy named Stefan who lived in the mansion at the other end of the field and zipped around in a beat-up wooden wheelchair. Most of the time she told Melanie everything, or almost everything. Everything that really mattered. They were more than mother and daughter, they were best friends. But she didn't tell her about Stefan or about the mansion.

And now it didn't matter. For all she knew, they'd be on their way to Alaska before the week was over.

# 5

"Yes, but you *must* have an address," the woman said patiently. "A legal address." She leaned toward Melanie across the scratched surface of the wooden desk, her plump brown hands clasped together. Oralia Ortiz, her name badge said. A beautiful name, Carolina thought. And she had let Carolina bring Crow into the office, so she had to be a beautiful person, too. But she didn't seem happy, at least not now. "In order to file for aid," Oralia Ortiz explained slowly and clearly, as if Melanie were a child or couldn't hear very well, "you have to have all the spaces filled in." She turned the form around so that Melanie could see what had been left blank.

"Well, there *is* an address . . ." Melanie said.

"Yes?"

"I . . . I just don't know what it is. It's a, well, it's this big . . . field." Melanie's eyes were wide. Carolina could tell that her mother knew she'd said the wrong thing.

"A field," repeated Mrs. Ortiz in a flat voice.

"That's where our bu . . . our *camper* is parked," said Melanie. "Just for the time being." Trinity kept trying to climb off Melanie's lap, and Melanie kept hauling her back up. "Just until I find a job."

Crow hopped onto the social worker's desk, snatched up a paper clip, and scuttled off.

"And the father of the children?" Oralia Ortiz asked. "I see you've left that blank as well?" It wasn't a question, it just sounded like one.

Melanie looked miserable. In all the years since Carolina had been born her mother had managed without asking anybody for help. Not even her own parents. But there were no jobs to be had in Santa Barbara, at least not any she could do. Just that morning they'd tried the last three restaurants within walking distance. Not only was there no work, not even washing dishes, there was no hope either. "Mostly we get the kids from the college," one manager said. "They're bright, they're quick . . ."

"I'm a good worker," Melanie pleaded. "I've got dozens of references, just let me show you!"

The manager began straightening things on the counter, brushing away invisible dust. "Sorry," he said. "I can see you need the work, but we just don't have anything." Then he brightened for a minute. "Does the little girl want a lollipop?" he asked. Insulted, Carolina refused the red Tootsie Roll pop, even though it was once her favorite. *Little girl?*

"You wouldn't want to work there anyway," she grumbled to Melanie as they left. The door closed behind them with a solid thud. "You wouldn't want to work for *him*."

Melanie's tears came from anger mixed with worry. "I'd work for anybody about now," she said. "I really would." She plunked down on a low rock wall outside the restaurant. Trinity let go of Melanie's hand and fell with a wet thump on her diapered bottom. "Honey, what'll we do?" It wasn't the first time Melanie had said those words in just that way.

"Don't worry, Melanie. Something will turn up."

How many times had she said that? She meant it, something always did turn up, but the words didn't sound as helpful as she wanted them to. "Maybe I could get a job. Delivering papers or something. If I had a bike . . ."

"Oh, sweetheart," Melanie sighed, picking herself up, handing Trinity to Carolina so that she could put the baby into her carrier, "you're already so much help. I don't know what I'd do without you. School is your job."

"Ugh," said Carolina.

Melanie's eyes narrowed, and she raised her right eyebrow. "You know what I'm going to say to that, don't you?" Blowing her nose, she stuffed the used tissue into her sleeve.

"I guess . . ."

"Well, it bears repeating, young lady." As they trudged back to the field and their bus, Melanie gave Carolina the lecture she'd heard more times than she could count, all about what happened to People Who Didn't Take Their

31

Schooling Seriously. "After all, look what happened to me," Melanie said.

Now Oralia Ortiz was lecturing Melanie. All about Women Who Refused to Disclose the Whereabouts of Their Children's Fathers.

"But I really don't know," protested Melanie. "Believe me, if I could find Trinity's father I wouldn't be here. It's hard to keep in touch, that's all. With him on the boat and us in the bus . . ."

"What bus?" When Oralia Ortiz frowned, her eyebrows met in the middle.

"Well, our school bus." Then she realized she'd given herself away. "It's like a camper. It's *just* like a camper, with beds and everything. Isn't it, Carolina?"

Carolina nodded solemnly. "Exactly," she said. She thought about Sergeant Carney. Maybe he could tell Oralia Ortiz how nice the bus was, how Melanie had worked so hard to make it a real home.

"I just need . . . *we* just need a little money for food . . ." mumbled Melanie, looking down into her hands, which were curled together and stuffed down into her skirt. When times were hard, Carolina could count on Melanie to say, "Well, at least we don't have to take welfare!" Now she was begging. It gave Carolina a sick feeling in her stomach.

"I'd better take Crow outside," she said. But it was too late. All down the side of Oralia Ortiz's desk, the side she couldn't see, were chalky-white streaks Crow had left behind.

As she closed the door, Carolina heard Oralia Ortiz in a weary voice say that there *were* some emergency funds and food stamps, but that Melanie had to find a permanent address. And she needed to find the father. Of *one* of the children, at least. On the way outside, Carolina read all the titles on the doors, looking for Child Protective Services. "Maybe the policeman made it up," she said to Crow. "Just to scare us." But saying it out loud didn't help her believe it.

Melanie and Carolina walked all the way back to the bus in silence. Trinity slept in her backpack, drooling, her face smushed against Melanie. Carolina tried to think of something to say that would make her mother feel better, that would give her hope again. She knew how proud Melanie was, how hard it was for her to ask for help. But in Carolina's throat was a stuck place that wouldn't let words through. She kept thinking about the kids at her last school who got the free lunches. Everybody knew who they were and stayed away from them, as if they carried some terrible disease. Would she have to get the free lunches now?

And she heard in her mind, as if for the very first time, the word "poor." We're *poor,* she said. I'm *poor.* It was like finding herself suddenly in a strange place, a foreign land, only to learn that she'd been there all along.

**6**

"Hey, I see you! Come out, come out wherever you are!" Stefan sang, his voice high and breathless with excitement.

Carolina peered out from behind the eucalyptus tree and waved. Stefan put down his binoculars. "Meet you downstairs!" he cried, and disappeared from the window.

The door opened slowly as Carolina came up to it. It was the tallest door she'd ever seen, except once on the front of a church. And there was Stefan in his old-fashioned wheelchair, wearing his goofy grin. Behind him stood a small round woman in a long black dress. "Lupe," Stefan explained. "Short for Guadalupe. She helps me out. This is Carolina," Stefan said. "And that bird on her shoulder, that's Crow."

"Please come in," said Lupe, stepping back. It looked to Carolina as if she bowed just a little, but how could that be? Why would a full-grown woman bow to an eleven-year-old girl?

"We'll give you the grand tour," said Stefan. "Nobody's home but us. Nothing unusual about that, is there, Lupe?"

It took Lupe's whole body to push the door closed. "Nothing unu-shual," she repeated in a soft accent, a smile on her smooth round face. She pushed Stefan's chair across the shiny tile-covered floor toward an archway, and Carolina followed along. They passed under ceilings so high and dark you could hardly see them. Crow could fly around in here, she thought. *If* he could fly.

And there, suddenly, was a room so big that Carolina's eyes couldn't take it all in at one time. At the far end was an immense stone fireplace. There were couches, huge ones, four of them, and fat comfy chairs you could curl up and sleep in, and rugs sort of scattered around as if it didn't really matter where they were or if you stepped on them. "The living room," Stefan announced. "Except nobody really lives in it." Over the fireplace was a beautiful painting of a young girl with light brown hair standing next to a shiny black horse. The girl wore riding clothes and a round black riding hat. One of her hands rested on the horse's neck, and she gazed out into the living room with such an air of confidence that Carolina couldn't take her eyes away.

"Next, the kitchen and all that dull stuff," Stefan said. "Then we'll do bedrooms and the rooms of the heir apparent. That's me," he said with a little chuckle.

Everything was silver in the kitchen: the stoves, the sinks, the countertops. They paraded around something Stefan called an "island." It was stuck in the middle of the floor and had a thick wooden top. "That's where Lupe does her stuff, huh, Lupe?" Along one wall was a row of knives, each one a little different than the one next to it, and shiny silver pots.

"Mother made pancakes in here once," Stefan said. "When she went on her domestic kick. But it was a disaster. Now she's into painting little boxes and doing her causes."

"Stefan . . ." said Lupe in a warning voice.

"Well, they're very *nice* little painted boxes," Stefan conceded. "And *very* important causes."

They headed across the tile floor once again and down a long, dimly lit hallway. Stefan came to a stop at three different rooms. "Bedroom, Guest," he announced at the first one, turning the knob and flinging open the door. Carolina barely got a look at a room that had rose-colored walls and dark fancy furniture before Stefan was off to the next one. "Bedroom, Guest," he said for the second one, which was pale gold with lots of lace. "Sitting room, Mother's," he said in the third doorway. "She really does sit in here. For hours sometimes. Doing nothing, staring into space. Weird!" Carolina thought so, too, but didn't say it. What would Melanie do with a sitting room? She surely wouldn't sit, at least not for long. Melanie was weird, too, but she always had something to do with her time.

At the end of the hallway was a set of stairs. "Heather's room," said Stefan nodding upward. "Locked." He quickly spun around and, Lupe in his wake, headed back down the hallway. He didn't stop until he'd recrossed the tiled entrance, gone back through the kitchen, and down another hallway. "That's all right, Lupe," he said. "You don't have to come up." To Carolina's great surprise a door slid open behind Stefan and an elevator waited to take them upstairs. A house with its very own elevator! She'd *have* to tell Melanie.

"Lupe's okay," Stefan explained as the elevator rose and jolted to a stop. "Only sometimes she tries to act like my mother, if you know what I mean."

Carolina wanted to ask why Lupe pushed his chair around when he could push it by himself, but it was hard to know how to ask questions like that without hurting a person's feelings.

The elevator door slid open and Stefan sailed off down another dark hallway. How many hallways did these rich people have? And if they were so rich, why didn't they have lights? Carolina hurried to catch up with Stefan.

An odor, not exactly awful but not exactly pleasant either, emerged from Stefan's room as he pushed open the door. It wasn't the kind of smell that belonged inside a house. And then Carolina saw what caused it. Stefan's room was full of cages, some stacked on top of others, some hanging from the ceiling. A stuffed owl stared down from a perch over a four-poster bed hung with mosquito netting. Snakeskins were tacked to the walls. Stefan's desk was piled with neatly labeled cigar boxes, and on a long, narrow table were cabinets with dozens of tiny drawers. Carolina slid open one of the drawers and peered inside. "Shark's teeth," Stefan said. "Petrified. Dug 'em up myself on a field trip. Come here, I'll introduce you to Frank."

"Frank?" She followed him over to a long, narrow cage. A dark furry animal with bright beady eyes emerged from a pile of dead leaves. Crow made a sound low in his throat that Carolina had never heard before.

"Frank's a ferret," said Stefan, but Frank was gone before Carolina could get a good look at him.

"What's wrong with him?" Carolina asked. She knelt down and peered into the cage.

"Nothing. Nothing's wrong with him. He's a ferret."

"Then why's he in a cage?"

Stefan got perfectly still, staring down at Carolina as if she had lost her mind. "He's being studied," he said at last. "It's just for now. I keep notes on all my animals. Usually I don't give them a name. Frank just got to be Frank somehow. Beats me . . . Look!" he said, excited again. "I was worried about this king snake. But you can see he's eating now."

Carolina looked through dusty glass at a loosely coiled black-and-white snake. Halfway down its long, slender body was a round bulge. "What's in there? A balloon?"

"A mouse," said Stefan. "I breed the mice myself over here. He wheeled across the room to a collection of wire-and-glass cages. They were filled with mice sleeping in piles or racing on little spinning wheels. Mice families, Carolina thought, though she didn't want to think it.

"I'm going to be a naturalist when I grow up," Stefan said. "World-famous, of course. It's never too soon to start, my father says. That's what he says about everything. *It's never too soon to start.* But it probably can be, don't you think? Too soon to start?"

Carolina said she didn't know what to think about that. She couldn't take her eyes away from a pile of wriggling, hairless, blind baby mice.

"You can take some home, if you want." Stefan offered. "Where do you live, anyway?"

Carolina bit back the fib that usually jumped out whenever she met someone new. "Closer than you think," she said.

"I figured, since you're always around here."

And then, she didn't quite know why, she told Stefan the truth. "We're living on your land," she said. "In your field."

Stefan whipped his chair around and stared up at Carolina. In the palm of his hand was a tiny mouse covered with light brown fur. "In *our* field?"

"In a bus," said Carolina, as miserable as Melanie had been at the welfare office. "I know we're trespassing, but—"

"You're kidding!"

Carolina slowly shook her head.

"Keen!" cried Stefan. "You actually live, like *every day*, in a bus?" He passed Carolina the mouse. It scurried around,

39

tickling the palms of her cupped hands. Crow had seen the mouse and watched it disappear. He fixed his eyes on Carolina's hand, as if to say, "I know it's in there! You can't fool me."

"We live in a school bus," said Carolina. "Me and Melanie and Trinity. Trinity's just a baby."

"Whoa!" said Stefan. "I never heard of anybody living, like actually *living,* inside a school bus. Is it fun?"

Carolina thought about it for a minute before answering. "Sometimes," she said at last. "When we go where we want."

"Yeah . . ." said Stefan, and Carolina could see the gears turning in his mind, the way they had in hers when she and Melanie found the old school bus and made plans for their first trip. Wheels made you free, Melanie said, but was it really true? Was it true for Stefan and his chair? Was it true for her and Melanie if they lived on somebody else's land?

"Can I come and see the bus?"

Carolina shrugged. "If you want."

"You're lucky my dad's out of the country. Jeez, would he raise a stink!" He held out his hand and Carolina dropped the little mouse into it. Crow hopped onto Stefan's shoulder, watching him put the mouse back into its cage.

"Is your father coming back soon?" She hoped Stefan wouldn't ask about *her* father. He was out of the country, too, she'd say, the way she always did.

"Yeah." His face clouded over for a minute. "Hey, maybe you could, like, pay rent or something. Then you could stay as long as you want."

"Yeah," said Carolina doubtfully. In her mind Stefan's father was eight feet tall and swallowed children the way the king snake swallowed mice.

Stefan flipped open one of his notebooks and began showing Carolina the detailed notes he took on the habits and behaviors of all his animals. Most had been injured in some way and could no longer forage for themselves. There was an atrium full of birds that he'd show Carolina next. "People bring me injured birds all the time," he said. "I'm getting famous already!"

"Stefan?" A tall, thin woman in a silvery gray dress appeared in Stefan's doorway. Her eyes were a paler shade of blue than Stefan's and she looked as if she was thinking about something very sad.

"Oh, hello, Mother," Stefan said cheerfully. "I was hoping you'd come home in time to meet my friend Carolina."

Stefan's mother stood motionless in the doorway. On her face was an expression Carolina couldn't read. She looked, Carolina thought, surprised. Maybe it was because of Crow. But why with all the other animals around would she be bothered by a bird? Then she seemed to wake up. Crossing the room, she extended her hand to Carolina as if Carolina were a grown-up. "So lovely to meet you, my dear," she said. She was very tall and stooped awkwardly over Carolina, that same intent look on her face. Then her eyes went to Crow and she smiled. "I see you share Stefan's fascination with wildlife."

Carolina's hand was stuck inside Stefan's mother's. She didn't seem to want to let go of it. "Stefan," she said at last, turning to her son, "did you ask Lupe to make you and your guest a snack? I'd say tea, but not everyone drinks tea in the afternoon as we do," she said for Carolina's benefit. Carolina took back her hand.

"I didn't ask her," Stefan said. "But you can, if you want. She can bring it up here."

Stefan's mother clasped her hands together and held them against her chest. "Oh, darling, you can't *eat* in here. How many times have I told you that? It's bad enough that you sleep in all this"—she waved a hand at the cages, the boxes, the draped bed—"all this clutter! We'll take tea in my sitting room, shall we? The light is perfect just now."

But Carolina blurted out that she had to leave, that she had to leave right now. If she'd had a watch, she'd have looked at it so they would know she wasn't just making it up. "I've got to baby-sit," she said, even though she knew Melanie had gone down to the welfare office to pick up the food stamps, carrying Trinity, as she always did, on her back.

Mrs. Crouch looked very disappointed. "Oh dear," she said. "Oh dear. Well, I do hope you'll come back. You live close by, do you?"

Carolina and Stefan exchanged a glance. This was just

the kind of question Carolina knew she'd be asked over tea. "Pretty close," she said. Stefan snickered.

"Well then, I'll see you out," said Stefan's mother, laying her hand against Carolina's back to lead her from the room. Crow ruffled his wings, glancing nervously behind him at the strange hand attached to the strange new person.

Carolina said goodbye to Stefan, who made her promise that she'd return in "not more than three days."

"We'll take the stairs, shall we?" Mrs. Crouch said as they left the room. Carolina descended the stairs, conscious of the hand that lingered lightly on her back. It wasn't as if she were being pushed out of the house. In fact, it seemed the other way around.

"Did Stefan show you the house?" Mrs. Crouch asked at the base of the stairs.

Carolina said that he had.

"Not Heather's room, of course."

"No, ma'am," said Carolina, but it was the room she was most curious about, a girl's room.

"We keep the room locked," said Mrs. Crouch, and smiled, but only with her mouth, a quick tight smile.

They crossed the entryway, Mrs. Crouch's heels clicking on the gleaming tile floor. Grasping a large iron ring, she pulled the great door open. The light outside made Carolina blink as if she'd been in a cave. "You will come back, won't you?" Stefan's mother said, leaning like a huge stork over Carolina and Crow as they passed.

"Sure," said Carolina. She looked up and saw Stefan waving from his window.

"Soon!" cried Mrs. Crouch. "We'll have tea next time," she called as Carolina hurried off across the patio. "Or whatever . . . whatever you'd like!"

Carolina's back itched in the place where Mrs. Crouch had kept her hand, but she couldn't reach back and scratch it, not with Mrs. Crouch watching. Besides, the itch was in that exact place you could never scratch yourself.

# 7

Carolina, barely awake, heard someone outside the bus calling her name. She popped her head up and peered out the window, and there was Stefan, wearing a green baseball cap with *Oakland* scrawled across it in gold letters. There were weeds stuck in the spokes of his wheels and Carolina wondered how long it had taken him to push the old chair all the way across the field and how hard that must have been. She guessed he was stronger than he looked.

Crow hopped ahead of her down the aisle, over the humps of Melanie and Trinity, who were still asleep.

"Hi!" said Carolina, stepping down from the bus into a cool, breezy morning. But the bus was colder, always, so it was good to be outside.

"Hi!" said Stefan.

Neither seemed to know what to say next.

Crow dropped from Carolina's shoulder to the ground. He picked up a pebble, then threw it down with a disgusted shake of his head. "He thinks everything's a treasure." Carolina shrugged.

"Maybe it is," said Stefan. "To him, anyway."

They watched Crow scurry off after something else that glinted brightly in the early-morning sunlight.

"Got any coffee?" Stefan did a half-wheelie in his chair, showing off.

"Coffee?"

"Sure. Don't you drink coffee?"

"Sometimes," said Carolina, not to be outdone. "Maybe Melanie will make us some when she gets up."

When Melanie appeared at the mention of her name, wrapped in her tattered blue bathrobe, Stefan was surprised. But Carolina wasn't. Melanie always slept "with one ear and one eye open." Within reach of her mattress was a metal baseball bat.

"This is Stefan, Melanie," said Carolina, and decided she might as well tell the rest. "It's his land we're living on."

Melanie's eyes widened.

"Well, not mine exactly," said Stefan, offering his hand the way his mother did, with a little lift of his chin. "My family's."

"Oh!" said Melanie. "Well!" Her welcoming smile turned into a crazy-looking grin.

"Stefan thinks we could pay his dad some rent or something," Carolina said.

Melanie's look said that Carolina had clearly lost her

marbles. They were living in a school bus precisely because they couldn't afford to pay rent.

"What a neat bus!" said Stefan, gazing up at the state stickers pasted on the windows. "You've been so many places! I've never been out of California. Well, except once to Hawaii. But I was just born, so it doesn't count. I don't remember a thing."

"Oh, I'd love to live in Hawaii!" cried Melanie, clapping her hands together as if she were ready right that moment to float the bus across the ocean. Nothing surprised Carolina when it came to her mother.

"Could I see the inside?" Stefan asked, his blue eyes bright with curiosity.

"Of course," said Melanie graciously. Then they all stared at each other and at Stefan's chair. "Well," she said then, "let's see what we can do." She led the way to the bus steps. "I know! You're light enough for the two of us, I think." She smiled reassuringly at Stefan, who didn't look convinced. "Grab your wrist like this," she told Carolina. "Then grab my wrist with your other hand. That's it."

"Aha!" croaked Stefan with a nervous giggle. "The old fireman's carry!"

Melanie and Carolina perched Stefan on their crossed arms, one of his arms around each of their necks. They waddled with him to the bus and lugged him onto the first step, already out of breath. Bumping their shoulders and skinning Stefan's right elbow, they made it to the top. "Watch your head!" warned Melanie, but Stefan bumped his head anyway. Then Carolina's left arm gave out and Stefan pitched toward her. "Timber!" he cried as they all went down, tumbling in a pile onto Melanie's bed. Trinity sent up a frightened howl, but Melanie, Carolina, and Stefan were laughing so hard that her cries were drowned out.

"Welcome to our home," said Melanie, sitting up and wiping her eyes. "You can drop in anytime!" And then they were laughing again, Carolina holding her side and gasping for breath.

"Been on any trips lately?" squealed Stefan, tears sliding down his pale cheeks.

"Stop!" cried Carolina. "Stop! I can't breathe!"

Melanie helped Stefan prop himself against her pillows while Carolina pointed out all the features of the bus. It was hard not to remember each detail of her tour of Stefan's house, the silver kitchen, the painted portraits of his family that went all the way back, he said, to the Mexican-American War, and she wondered what he could be thinking. His goofy grin was back, and his legs were splayed out in front of him.

She took a chance. "So what do you think?"

"Turtles," he said at once.

"Huh?"

"Well, I was thinking about turtles. You know, about how self-sufficient they are," Stefan said, as if he was thinking out loud. "Carrying their house around with them, ducking inside when the weather gets bad or when they get threatened by predators and stuff. They don't need anything but what they carry with them. Kind of like, you know, you on this bus."

Melanie bestowed on Stefan her most dazzling smile. "Well, we're hardly self-sufficient," she said, glancing from Stefan to Carolina, "but we have everything we need, don't we, honey?"

Everything we need, thought Carolina. Was it true? They had a pee bucket that had to be emptied every morning, a washbowl instead of a shower, sleeping bags for blankets, flashlights for lamps. They got their water in gas-station bathrooms, filling plastic jug after plastic jug until somebody ran them off.

The bus looked awfully small to Carolina just then. She thought that if people kept telling Melanie how neat the bus was, they'd have to live in it forever. Until she'd read every one of the ninety-seven books. Until she was old.

"Oh!" cried Stefan, slapping his forehead, "I almost forgot. Mother sent this." He pulled a small envelope out of his back pocket. "It's an invitation to her charity tea. On Saturday."

Melanie, a tiny frown between her eyes, opened the cream-colored envelope. Inside was a folded-over note. After she'd read it, Melanie ran the tip of her finger over the gold-embossed monogram on the front. "Well," she said quietly, "that's very nice. A tea."

"We can go, can't we?"

Melanie looked right through Carolina. "Hmmm?"

"We can go, right?"

"Well," said Melanie. "I don't know . . ."

"It's pretty boring," said Stefan quickly. "You don't have to come. The food's pretty good and stuff, but everybody just sits around and yaks. Plus they bring all these old clothes, gowns and fancy dresses they don't want anymore. I think they should just give money, but Mother doesn't agree."

"I guess people get pretty dressed up, huh? For a tea . . ." Melanie smiled. She liked Stefan, Carolina could tell. He'd won her over with that stuff about the turtles.

"You could wear your black dress," Carolina said. They'd found the ankle-length black sundress at a thrift shop, but nobody would have to know that.

"We'll see," said Melanie.


"A charity tea!" said Melanie when Stefan had gone. "I guess that means he hasn't told his parents where we live." Melanie stood with her hands on her hips, gazing down the center aisle of the bus.

Carolina was working on Crow's only trick, the one where he stepped neatly from the back of one of her hands to the back of the next until they both got tired. "No, I guess not."

Melanie sighed. "Well, they'll have to know."

"Why?"

"Because if they find out some other way, if somebody else tells them . . . well, we'll look like . . . Well, we won't look very respectable, that's all."

"Guess what, Melanie?" said Carolina, sounding to herself very grown-up. "We aren't."

"What?" Up went Melanie's eyebrows.

"Respectable. We aren't, like, *respectable*."

"Get out the dictionary, young lady," ordered Melanie.

"What for?"

"Just do as I say. If you're going to throw my words back at me, you'd better know what they mean!"

Carolina sighed her most dramatic sigh. She put Crow down and picked up the big Webster's. "I know what it *means*," she muttered. But Melanie stood over Carolina with her arms crossed while Carolina thumbed through the pages. *"Meriting respect or esteem,"* she read when she'd found the word, *"worthy."*

"And respect? Go ahead. Look it up."

Carolina's finger went up the page. *"To show consideration for,"* she read in a bored voice, *"to honor—"*

"And don't you think we deserve respect, young lady?" Melanie asked. "Consideration?"

"I guess . . ." When Melanie got wound up, it was better to agree with everything she said. Otherwise, she went on and on until your head ached.

"You *guess*?" Melanie sighed. She squatted beside Carolina on the bus floor. "Honey, respect doesn't have to do with how much money somebody has. Respect, *respectable*, is for what you are inside." She knocked her chest with her fist for emphasis. "What you're made of as a person, you know?" She tilted Carolina's chin so that Carolina couldn't look anywhere but into her eyes, which were all sorts of colors, yellow and green and gray, and serious as anything. Then she sighed, a heavy deep sigh, and stood up. "Well, this bus doesn't look very respectable at the moment, I'll give you that. Housecleaning time!" she cried, dusting her hands together.

Carolina groaned.

"Out with the mattresses! Down with the curtains!" Melanie whipped the red-and-white-checkered tablecloth off the table and stuffed it into the laundry bag. "The whole time your friend was here—Stefan—all I could see was finger smudges on the windows."

They stripped the beds. They pulled and pushed all three mattresses out the door and laid them in the sun. While Melanie swept and scrubbed the floor, Carolina washed the windows, using their precious bottled water sparingly. Trinity chewed on an old sock that was supposed to be the dust rag. From his perch on the steering wheel, Crow supervised.

Carolina worked pretty hard, considering that no matter which side of the windows she was on, the dirt was always on the other side. Which was always the way with windows. When she finished one whole row and moved to the other, she saw someone striding across the field toward the bus. "Melanie?"

Melanie turned and looked where Carolina pointed. Then she was gone. Out the folding door and racing across the field, her golden curls bouncing. In a flash she was in Red's arms, her head against his chest, his red head resting on her curls. Except for no music, it was just like in the movies. Carolina went outside and watched her mother and Trinity's father strolling arm in arm toward the bus. Red ducked his head and said something to Melanie. Laughing, she pressed her head harder against his chest. Red had found them. He'd finally found them.

"Hey, kiddo!" cried Red, catching Carolina under the armpits and sailing her in a wide circle, her hair flying. He smelled of salt water and fish guts, just as Carolina remembered. "I guess you're too big for that now," he said when he set her down. Carolina guessed, sadly, that he was probably right. Still, she loved sailing in the air, weightless. "Where's the baby?"

"Trinity," said Carolina.

"Hey! You don't think I'd forget that, do you? Didn't I name her myself?" Red was a big square man with a booming voice that came from having to yell louder than the boat engine.

Melanie ducked inside the bus and came out carrying Trinity, who rubbed her nose and eyes at the same time with her fat fists, then buried her head shyly in Melanie's neck.

Had Red forgotten? He hadn't named Trinity, Melanie had. She named her after the town Trinity was born in, just like Carolina was named for her state. The trouble with Red was that he never stayed around long enough to get the facts straight. But Carolina could see that Melanie had already forgotten all the bad things about Red.

After a while Red went back to his boat for his guitar and

the makings of a special dinner. As night fell, they cele-
brated being together again. Red built a fire inside a ring of
stones with a place to set his cooking pot. The big black-
ened pot was filled with water and a handful of Red's "secret spices." When the seasoned water began to bubble, he
threw all kinds of things into it: crab claws, mussels, a lob-
ster tail. Then he gutted a fish and threw that in, too, head
and all. Fish eyes stared up from the boiling broth. "Best
part," Red always said. He pretended to eat the eyes, but
never really did.

As he cooked, Red told the story of how he came to find
them, how he'd checked in every single harbor city
straight down the coast before finding the old fisherman
who remembered "the curly-headed lady with the kids."
"Monterey, Pismo, San Luis . . ." He frowned, trying to remember where else he might have looked. The fisherman
told Red where to find the bus, and here he was. But his
story didn't make much sense to Carolina. Wouldn't he
have told them exactly where to go if he really wanted to
find them?

Red sat on Melanie's mattress, Trinity in the scoop of
his crossed legs, telling stories about the places he'd been,
how light the catch was, how hard it was to make a living
on the sea. Melanie never looked anywhere but his face.
Her eyes shone as if she'd just won something special,
some contest.

Carolina felt two ways at once about Red, about Red
coming back. He made Melanie happy, and when Melanie
was happy, everything in the world seemed right. In the

glow of Red's fire, joined together in the night, they seemed like a family. But it wouldn't last. Red wouldn't stay. He never promised to, and he never would.

After they finished their steaming bowls of fisherman's stew, Red settled down with his guitar. Crow, fascinated by the guitar's shiny strings, waddled up and plucked one, then leaped straight up into the air, his wings spread, when the sound came out. They all laughed. Crow stalked away, embarrassed.

Red played all the songs they knew, "On Top of Old Smoky," "Tom Dooley," "Itsy Bitsy Spider" for Trinity, who pushed her fingers together just the way she was supposed to and grinned with all six of her teeth. Melanie, who couldn't carry a tune, sang the loudest, as if her heart was finally full.

After a while, Carolina grew sleepy. She lay down on her mattress, gazing up at the stars and the lemon-rind moon. She didn't know just when her eyes closed, but they were closed when Melanie whispered that "the kids" were asleep. She listened as Melanie scooped up Trinity and carried her inside the bus. She heard Red lift Trinity's mattress. Then she heard Melanie and Red come back outside. She peeked through her eyelids and saw them kissing. Then they broke apart and just looked at each other with silly faces.

"Carolina?" Melanie was somewhere over Carolina's head, between her mattress and the stars. "Time to go inside, sweetheart."

But Carolina pretended to be fast asleep.

"Okay, sleepyhead, you're next," Red said, hefting Carolina into his arms as if she weighed nothing.

"You don't have to carry her, Red," Melanie protested. "She's a grown girl. Come on, Carolina." But Carolina, her cheek against Red's scratchy sweater, her long legs dangling, breathed in the sea air, the salt water, the fish guts, and wouldn't have opened her eyes for a million dollars.

# 8

The charity tea had already begun by the time Carolina and Melanie came hurrying across the field, Trinity bumping up and down in her pack. Women in silky flower-printed dresses sat beneath blue-and-white-striped umbrellas at round tables set with vases of flowers and crystal glasses. There were children, too, mostly girls, and they were dressed like their mothers, like miniature versions of their mothers. The mansion loomed over everything, unsmiling. Stopping short of the patio, Melanie grabbed Carolina's hand to slow her down. "What a house! How do I look? Do I look okay? Is there lipstick on my teeth?"

"You look fine," said Carolina, still in what Melanie called a "snit." Melanie had made her wear the green plaid dress they had bought for school, the one Carolina gave in on because Melanie was making such a scene in the thrift shop.

Carolina never wore dresses, never. She wasn't used to having all that air up around her underpants. You couldn't do anything in a dress. You couldn't do the bars at school, you couldn't run. But Melanie told her that sixth grade would be different. She'd be going to a middle school with seventh- and eighth-graders. There wouldn't be swings and bars. She was growing up, that's all there was to it.

She might as well have told Carolina she was going to jail.

Melanie smoothed Carolina's hair back from her face. She'd yanked a comb through it hours before, Carolina yelling for all she was worth while Crow hopped nervously just out of reach, as if he might be next. "It's time for you to do your own hair, you know," Melanie had said. "You need to start taking care of yourself."

"I do take care of myself!" Carolina had snatched the comb out of Melanie's hand, insulted.

"You know what I mean, Caro. You're getting to be a young lady—"

"Yuck!" said Carolina.

"Pretty soon you'll be begging me for clothes money. Money for nail polish and hair spray."

"Wanna bet?"

Then they started arguing about the plaid dress. Melanie said you couldn't wear jeans to a tea party. Carolina said she didn't know there were rules about what to wear to tea parties. But Melanie said there were, plenty of them. They just weren't written down. Then Melanie said she wouldn't go unless Carolina wore a dress. The green plaid dress was the only one she had. Pulling the thing over her head made her want to throw up, but now she saw that Melanie was right. All the ladies were wearing dresses—beautiful dresses with flowing skirts. Some of the women even wore gloves.

Carolina shook loose of Melanie's hand. "Come on," she said. "You've got the invitation, right?"

"They don't make you show it, Caro."

Carolina stopped, horrified. "How do you know? You have it, don't you?" What did Melanie know about the rules for tea parties? They could get sent back, right in front of everybody.

Carolina saw Mrs. Crouch detach herself from a group of chattering ladies and cross the patio. "Here she comes!" cried Carolina. "Hurry up, find the invitation!"

"Carolina!" trilled Mrs. Couch. "I'm so delighted that you're here. And you even brought the bird. My, *my*!" She squinted at Crow as if she wasn't sure he was really there on Carolina's shoulder. "And *this*," she said, "*this* must be your lovely mother." She clasped Melanie's hand in both of hers. Her pale blue eyes took in everything in a quick sweep: Melanie's black sundress with the bare shoulders and scoop neck, Melanie's gold-plated hoop earrings, her sandals, which were covered with dust from crossing the field. Trinity peeked over Melanie's shoulder. Her eyes were very wide. "Come," Mrs. Crouch said. "I'll find you a table." She walked them around the outside of the patio to an empty table at the far edge. Next to the table were racks of women's clothes smelling of mothballs. "Would you like a mimosa?" she asked Melanie.

Melanie nodded quickly. "Yes, thank you."

"I'll send Rodolfo right over," said Mrs. Crouch.

"What's a mimosa?" whispered Carolina as Stefan's mother disappeared into the crowd. Somebody was playing a violin somewhere off in the bushes while the ladies munched on tiny pieces of food, a squiggle of cheese on a cracker, doll-sized sandwiches with the crusts cut off.

"I don't know!" Melanie laughed. "It just sounded good. Look at all these gorgeous dresses!" She reached for a gown with glittering blue sequins.

"Don't touch it!" cried Carolina. Luckily, no one had seen.

"Silly!" said Melanie, but she kept her hands to herself after that and made sure Trinity did, too.

Rodolfo, a very serious man in a short white jacket and black bow tie, brought Melanie her mimosa on a little round tray. She took a sip and frowned. "Orange juice," she said. "Mostly."

"Is it booze?" Melanie got pretty silly on a glass of wine.

"Tastes like it."

Carolina got something red with a cherry in it. When another man came with a tray of tiny sandwiches, Melanie took three, quickly wrapping two in a paper napkin for later.

Carolina thought it might be time to faint, but she'd never fainted before and didn't know how. So she sat with a face the color of her drink and tried to act normal.

From a small platform at the far end of the patio Mrs. Crouch rang a little silver bell. When she got the attention of the ladies, she thanked them all for coming and for donating their clothes. Then she started talking about the "battered women" and how grateful they would be. Carolina tried to ask Melanie who the battered women were, but Melanie shushed her. "We live in a very generous community," Mrs. Crouch said. "Full of kind hearts and gentle people! I applaud you all." She clapped her hands and the ladies joined in.

"Well?" said Carolina.

"Well what?"

"What's a battered woman? What was Mrs. Crouch talking about?"

Melanie explained about the shelters that took in women whose husbands treated them badly, who beat them up and sometimes hurt their children as well. The shelter kept the men away and helped the women get back on their feet.

Carolina thought about that for a while. It was nice what Mrs. Crouch was doing, but it still didn't make a lot of sense to Carolina. "That's pretty sad," she said, "but what are the battered women going to do with, you know"—she nodded toward the racks of fancy clothes—"with evening gowns?"

"Oh, I don't think the clothes are for them," Melanie said. "They'll have a rummage sale or something. The money will go to the shelter."

They sat for what seemed a very long time eating little sandwiches and tiny squares of cake. Sometimes one of the ladies from another table would turn her head and pretend to be looking somewhere past Crow, who was perched on Carolina's shoulder or strutting around the table in search of crumbs. Then that lady would turn to another lady, who would wait for a little while before she, too, turned and pretended not to look.

After a while the ladies started to leave, but Carolina wanted to wait for Stefan, who'd promised to show her his atrium. Instead, Mrs. Crouch came back. "So sorry to have deserted you," she said. "But with all these people to attend to . . . Well, you have to say *something* to *everybody* or they're miffed! You know how it is."

Melanie said that she did, but of course she didn't. How could she?

"Come inside, won't you? We'll have a little chat."

She led the way past the racks of clothes and into the house. Stefan was waiting in the entry. "What did I tell you?" he said. "Boring, huh? And what about all those stinky clothes? Whew! Come on." He motioned the way to the elevator. "You never got to see the lizards or the birds."

"Just one moment, young man," said Mrs. Crouch. "I want you to take Carolina's mother into the sitting room, but first I'm sure she'd love to see Grandmother Crouch's china collection."

Stefan, who was halfway across the tile floor, turned, a puzzled expression on his face. "Huh?"

Mrs. Crouch's eyebrows went straight up. "Pardon *me*, young man?"

"Oh, I'm sorry, Mother." Stefan grinned. "You surprised me." He sat straight up in his chair and raised his chin a little, just like his mother. "It would be my great pleasure to show Mel—to show *Carolina's mother*—Grandmother Crouch's exquisite china collection."

"Stefan, be careful . . ." warned his mother with a raised finger.

"Yes, ma'am." Carolina could see how hard he was trying to be serious. "This way, please," he said to Melanie. And off they went.

Mrs. Crouch put her hand on Carolina's back, in that exact same place. "Come this way," she said. "There's something I'd like you to see."

Carolina followed Stefan's mother down the hallway past the two bedrooms, Guest, and Mrs. Crouch's sitting room. They turned at the end of the hall, went up two flights of stairs, and came to a stop at a closed door. Mrs. Crouch reached up to the collar of her dark blue dress and tugged at a pink ribbon that was tied around her neck. At the end of the ribbon was a key. She pulled the ribbon over her hair, which was mostly gray and rolled on the top of her head like a doughnut. Carolina, her heart beating for some reason she didn't yet know, watched Stefan's mother fit the key into the door and push it open. She stepped aside. "Go on in," she said.

Carolina did as she was told. "Wow!" she gasped as she sunk into fluffy white carpet. A single word was all she could manage. The pale pink room was flooded with sunlight. Against the far wall was a white four-poster bed. From the top of the bed hung lacy white curtains that were tied to the posts with pink velvet ribbons. A dozen pillows were piled against the headboard, pink velvet pillows, pillows embroidered with roses or trimmed with lace. "Heather loved pink," Mrs. Crouch said quietly, standing behind Carolina. Then she crossed the room to a set of double doors. "Just look at how much pink is in this closet."

When Mrs. Crouch opened the doors and switched on the light, it was as if the sun had followed them into the room-sized closet, bathing everything, dresses, shoes, shelves full of sweaters, in a fuzzy warm light. Speechless, Carolina reached for a pink patent-leather shoe, one of dozens of shoes of every color and style imaginable.

"About your size, I should think," Mrs. Crouch said. Carolina set the shoe down as if it were on fire.

Mrs. Crouch turned and faced the room again. "I didn't know what to do with all these books, and of course her horse collection . . ." She crossed the room and stood staring at a tiny glass horse with a flying tail and mane. "So I just . . . I just . . . left everything as it was." She turned to Carolina, smiling that same tight, sad smile. Carolina guessed there were a hundred horses on the shelf, a whole herd.

"Would you like to stay here for a while?" said Mrs. Crouch with wide wet eyes. "I mean, *play* in here. Just while . . . while your mother and I are talking."

"Sure," said Carolina, not just because she was curious about the beautiful room and everything in it, but because her being there seemed so important to Stefan's mother.

"Everything's just as it was," she repeated, her blue eyes fixed on Carolina's face. "It's almost as if . . ." She seemed to fade away, then caught herself and smiled her sad little smile. "We'll be in the sitting room," she said as she left the room. "Come down whenever you'd like, my dear."

Carolina gave Mrs. Crouch a few minutes to get down the stairs and went straight back to the closet. Something had caught her eye in the middle of all that pink. She looked down a rack that was filled with dresses, and sure enough, there it was. Carolina pulled a black velvet dress from among its frilly cousins. It was a plain dress, with a simple row of black buttons down the front, and it was soft as Trinity's stuffed rabbit. Carolina walked to the back of the closet. Standing at a mirror that covered the whole wall, she held the black dress against her body, blotting out every inch of the horrid green plaid. Never before had she wanted a dress. It felt wrong somehow to want this one. But she did. She wanted it so badly her throat ached.

She slipped a shiny black shoe from among six pairs of black shoes. The one she chose had a bow on the front, but aside from that it was okay. Feeling like Cinderella, looking behind her to make sure Mrs. Crouch or Heather herself hadn't returned and was staring at her from the open door of the closet, she slipped her foot into the shoe. A little big, maybe a whole size.

So she wasn't Cinderella, after all. A glimpse in the mirror at the plaid dress reminded her of who she was and where she belonged.

How would it feel to actually *be* Heather?

She stayed awhile longer in the silent room full of sunshine, trying not to touch everything she saw, but her fingers couldn't help themselves. Heather's Teddy bears looked extra cuddly, the Barbies needed to stand up if they were sitting down or sit down if they were standing up, the play jewelry needed to be tried on, every piece, and the horses needed to run. Even Heather's books in their colorful jackets invited Carolina to open them.

She tried not to think about Heather and of how she herself would feel if Heather were back in the bus right now going through *her* things, her treasure box, her box of favorite T-shirts, opening *Swiss Family Robinson* with the picture of her father.

She was putting *Black Beauty* back on the shelf when Stefan appeared at the door. "How did you get up here?" she said. It still amazed her how fast Stefan zipped around the huge house.

Stefan said he'd come up the service elevator, that he was the only one who ever used it. It was for "the help," he explained, but Lupe didn't trust elevators. "Your mother and my mother are still yakking it up downstairs," he said.

"What are they talking about?" Was Melanie telling Mrs. Crouch about the bus? What would Mrs. Crouch say? Would she let them stay?

"You wanna listen in? You can hear through the heater grate in my room." He grinned mischievously. "I do it all the time."

They went down one elevator, up another, and got to

Stefan's room in no time at all. Sure enough, when Carolina put her ear to the grate, she could hear Mrs. Crouch's sad voice plain as a radio.

". . . an accident," she said. "One of those horrible, unavoidable things. Heather was an excellent rider, but the horse was young, high-spirited. She died instantly in the fall."

The girl in the picture! Stefan's sister.

"Oh, my dear," crooned Melanie, and Carolina was certain that her mother had reached over and touched Mrs. Crouch on her hand or arm. She'd have wanted to hug her, but Carolina didn't think Melanie would do that to Stefan's mother.

"Well, it's been four years," said Mrs. Crouch. "And things, they say, get easier with time." Up through the heater grate came a deep sigh. "Stefan's a joy, of course. So intelligent. So full of himself."

"That's me!" whispered Stefan. "Full of myself!" He covered his mouth to keep from laughing loud enough for the mothers to hear.

"I thought when he was born—his poor little body the way it was!—that I had surely experienced the greatest tragedy a mother could face. But he's alive. There are things he can't do, but he's *alive.* I never guessed that my darling girl—" She broke off. A cup clattered lightly against a saucer and Carolina realized that they'd never had tea at the "tea." "But surely," Mrs. Crouch continued, "you've had troubles of your own. Living as you do on that bus . . ."

Carolina's breath stuck in her throat. Mrs. Crouch *knew*!

"Oh, we manage," Melanie said quickly. "Really, it's not so terrib—" She broke off.

"Trinity! Don't touch, sweetheart."

"But for *Carolina*," Mrs. Crouch urged, as if Melanie had forgotten that she had an eleven-year-old daughter. "She's darling! And so bright. She deserves every opportu— Well, I'm sure you know she's a very special girl." Carolina squirmed. She didn't dare look up at Stefan, who was trying to hear by leaning down as far as he could from his chair.

"Yes, she is," said Melanie glumly. "She certainly is."

Both women sighed.

"And with the baby and all . . . No job . . ."

Had Melanie told Mrs. Crouch *everything*?

Carolina listened to the teacups rattle. Someone—Carolina guessed it was Melanie—blew her nose. Was Melanie crying? In front of Stefan's mother?

"She could stay here, you know," said Mrs. Crouch so quietly that Carolina wasn't sure she'd heard the words right.

*"Trinity?"* said Melanie.

Carolina's heart went into her throat. Mrs. Crouch wanted to keep the baby!

"Oh no, my dear," said Mrs. Crouch in a soothing voice. "I meant Carolina. While you get settled with Trinity's father."

Settled? What was Stefan's mother talking about?

"Or perhaps for the school year. Longer, if you'd like.

Carolina could go to Country Day with Stefan. It's an excellent school. If Carolina wanted to stay, of course."

"Is she asking if you could stay here?" whispered Stefan.

"Shhh! Wait!" Carolina pressed her ear harder against the grate and finally heard Melanie's voice.

"That's very kind of you, Mrs. Crouch—"

"Madeleine," reminded Stefan's mother.

"Madeleine," repeated Melanie. "I just couldn't go to Oregon without Carolina, without my *daughter*. I mean, I can't imagine—!"

*Oregon?* Who was going to Oregon? Carolina held her breath to keep from yelling through the vent. How was it that Mrs. Crouch knew things that she, Melanie's own daughter, didn't know?

"Well, of course, it would be difficult . . ."

"Impossible!" said Melanie.

"Did she say no?" hissed Stefan.

"Of course she said no!" Carolina hissed back.

"I know how you feel, my dear," said Stefan's mother. "I wouldn't have suggested it except for Carolina."

Neither woman spoke for a while. Then Melanie started up again in a voice that said she'd been thinking real hard. "Well," she said. "I *know* she deserves more than I can give her right now. I *know* that." Another nose blow. "I do the best I can. It isn't easy."

"Of course it isn't easy, my dear. And children don't know, do they? How hard it is."

Trinity was getting fussy. It was time to go home.

"No, of course they don't. Not really. How can they? But Carolina's a great help," said Melanie quickly. "You'd be surprised at the things she can do. She shops, does laundry, baby-sits . . . everything!"

"Well, that's the point, I suppose," said Stefan's mother. "When I think of the wonderful life Heather had. What a happy, *carefree* child she was! Well, I just thought . . . but perhaps it was wrong of me—"

"No!" protested Melanie. "Please don't think I'm not grateful. I know Carolina should go to a good school. I know she'd love to live in a house like this. What little girl wouldn't? I'm just being selfish." She sighed deeply. "I should let her stay here, I *should*. Just for a while."

"Yes, of course. Just for a while."

"While we got settled, Red and me. Maybe we could find a little house for the four of us in Oregon."

"I'm sure you could. If you didn't have to worry about finding a school right away for Carolina. If it were just the three of you."

Carolina felt hot tears creep into her eyes. She took her ear away from the heater grate and sat up.

"What did they say?" asked Stefan, his blue eyes wide.

But Carolina couldn't answer just then without crying, and she didn't want to do that in front of Stefan, so she just hung her head for a while and picked at her thumbnail. Stefan didn't move. The mice scurried around in their cages. Crow, sitting on the windowsill looking out, ruffled his wings. Finally, Carolina looked up. "We're moving to Oregon," she said. "Melanie didn't even tell me!"

"Bummer," said Stefan. "Maybe she was going to tell you and, you know, forgot or something. Maybe she was going to do it later. As a surprise."

"She knows I don't want to go. I *hate* Red. And besides, Crow belongs here, where he was born. He can't even fly yet."

"Well, you and Crow could live with us. I think it would be great, I mean, if you did . . ." His voice trailed off and he shrugged, embarrassed.

"I *belong* with Melanie, Stefan. She *needs* me." But a voice inside said, *It would be easier. It would be easier without me . . .*

71

# 9

The next day Carolina moped around the back of the bus in her "room" with Crow while Melanie moped around in front with Trinity. Carolina thought about telling her mother what she knew, what she had heard through the heater grate. But she couldn't. Melanie would be furious. She trusted Carolina not to do sneaky things. And besides, what difference would it make?

She watched Melanie dump the money can onto her mattress and count the change. "Don't!" cried Melanie when Trinity put a quarter into her mouth. It wasn't like Melanie to yell at Trinity, ever.

*It would be easier . . .*

Hadn't Melanie said once that Carolina could eat like a horse?

———

That night she had two nightmares.

One turned out to be real.

In the first one Carolina found herself standing just inside the high, rounded archway of Stefan's living room. It was night and she was all alone. She knew this the way you know things in dreams, even though she couldn't see the rest of the house.

The air was very still in the living room, the room Stefan said nobody lived in. The only sound came from the big brass pendulum of a grandfather clock that clicked the minutes back and forth. Covered with white sheets, the furniture looked like heaped-up snow or crouching ghosts. Carolina stood in the archway and stared at the portrait above the fireplace, the portrait of the girl with the horse, the girl she now knew was Heather. It seemed she could look nowhere else, that her eyes would go only there. And then, while she watched, something moved. A hand, an eyelid . . .

She stumbled backward, all her breath frozen in her chest. Before Carolina's unbelieving eyes, Heather came alive. First her eyes, which were fixed and painted, began to glow; her hand with the little whip lifted just so. Then, as Carolina stood paralyzed in the archway, Heather daintily kicked one tall black boot right out of the portrait and stepped down onto the mantel of the stone fireplace.

Carolina awoke covered with sweat, her heart knocking so hard she could hear it. "Melanie?" The bus was flooded with moonlight. But Melanie's bed was empty, the covers thrown back as if she was in a hurry to leave her bed.

Carolina got up and made her way to the front of the bus, past the sleeping Trinity, into the driver's seat, her heart beating and beating. The moon cast tree shadows across the field, stretched out like reaching fingers. And then she saw the people.

At first they were just that, any two people. But then she knew, because she knew the shape of her mother the way she knew each line in her own palms, each freckle on her nose, that one of them was Melanie. The other, the big one, was Red.

They were dancing, she thought, dancing in the light of the full moon. Melanie would do that, and maybe Red would, too. If he was drinking he would. They were holding each other's arms and pulling, like a tug-of-war game. More like a game than a dance. But then Melanie went down, hard, and Carolina knew it wasn't a game. She grabbed Melanie's baseball bat, cranked open the door, and hit the ground running. As she raced toward them, she saw Red turning to leave and Melanie grabbing his arm to pull him back. He shoved her away, and she stumbled to the ground.

"Don't you touch my mother!" Carolina yelled. She headed for Red, the bat behind her shoulder, the way you were supposed to, like a boy, and she swung at his legs with all her strength. Red grabbed the bat in mid-swing. Shaking it from Carolina's hands, he flung it away, his eyes red and watery, full of angry confusion.

"Caro!" Melanie cried.

Red brought his big hands up to his forehead and raked them through his hair. He didn't smell of fish and the sea tonight. He smelled like booze. He staggered backward in his big boots. "Now look what you've done! You can't just leave well enough alone, can you? I told you I'll get some money, only don't bug me about it!"

"Go on back to the bus, sweetheart," urged Melanie, giving Carolina a quick squeeze and letting her go again. "Everything's fine. Don't worry. We just had a little argument."

Red gave a disgusted little wave of his hand and turned away. "Red!" cried Melanie. "Don't go. Don't leave. I'm sorry!" But Red kept on walking, his shape getting smaller, his shadow growing longer, until he and his shadow disappeared altogether.

Carolina clung to Melanie, pulled her back, stood fast in the way of her going after Red. "Oh, Caro!" wept Melanie. "I blew it. I said all the wrong things. I made him so mad." She shook her head, remembering whatever it was she had said and wishing the words back.

"But he pushed you!" Carolina cried. "I saw him!"

"Oh, sweetie. He didn't mean to hurt me."

"He did! I saw him!"

"Come on," sighed Melanie at last. "He's not coming back. Let's go inside."

"Put the bar inside the door," said Carolina when Melanie had cranked the door closed.

"Don't I always?"

"He could break a window."

"Red? Honey, he wouldn't do that." But Carolina had seen, out on the shadowed moonlit field, a different Red than the one her mother meant. She never wanted to see that Red again.

"Why didn't you tell me about Oregon?"

Melanie didn't say anything for a little while. She didn't even seem to be breathing. "I would have, honey. You know that. I just knew you'd be upset about leaving. Red says the fishing's much better up there. Santa Barbara's all fished out."

"But you won't go now, right? You won't go with him!"

"Oh, Caro," sighed Melanie. "You just don't understand. Maybe someday you will. When you're in love with somebody. When you have a baby with somebody you love."

"Maybe I won't," said Carolina.

"Won't what?"

"Maybe I won't have babies. It isn't easy if you have children."

"What isn't easy? What are you talking about?" Melanie yawned and climbed under her comforter.

"You know, buying food and stuff. *Living* . . ."

"Come here, silly," said Melanie, and Carolina crawled into Melanie's bed as if she were six years old, when last she'd slept snuggled next to her mother. They lay on their backs wide-awake, listening to Trinity's tiny baby snores, to the bus that always talked in the night in the language of buses, which calmed people although they could not understand.

"Melanie?"

"Mmmm?"

Carolina didn't know how to say it any other way than the way she'd just learned. "Are you a battered woman?"

"Caro!" cried Melanie. "Of course not! Of course I'm not a battered woman! What an idea!" Her laugh sounded more like a bark, and Carolina knew she had shocked Melanie. And maybe that wasn't such a bad thing.

"Tell him not to come back," Carolina pleaded.

"But . . . I don't want to do that, honey. I love Red. He's Trinity's daddy. How can I tell him not to come back?"

"We don't need him," said Carolina.

And the tears that were stuck inside Carolina, inside her fear, came flooding to the surface. She buried her head against Melanie and sobbed.

Melanie rocked Carolina against her in the old way, the way Carolina had been rocked years before. She hummed an old song that was really a prayer, one Carolina hadn't heard since she was a little girl. "Look, Caro," said Melanie after a while. "Look at Crow."

He was perched on the steering wheel, a black silhouette against the moonlit windshield. "He's guarding us. He's our watchcrow." But for some reason that just made Carolina cry harder.

# 10

Red stayed away for several days. Then, as if nothing at all had happened, he came whistling across the field. "How about a ride on the *Mary Louise*?"

Melanie looked at Carolina. Carolina looked away. She loved the *Mary Louise*. So much that she thought she might someday become a fisherman (Melanie said fisher-*person*). After she became a veterinarian, of course, and an artist.

Red stood with his big arms crossed over his chest, looking pretty satisfied with himself. "Weather's perfect," he said. "Tomorrow, first light, I'm going after halibut. Then it's work, work, work." He looked straight at Carolina. "It's your only chance," he said.

"Come on, Caro," coaxed Melanie, and Carolina could hear how much it would mean to her mother if she said yes, if she gave Red another chance. She chewed on a piece of broken-off thumbnail. It wasn't up to her. *They* could go, Melanie and Trinity.

"Last chance," he said.

"If Stefan can come," Carolina muttered. "And Crow."

"Sure thing!" cried Red, and she could hear the relief in his voice. "Bring all your friends."

*All* her friends? Didn't he know that Stefan was the only friend she had? And Crow, of course. But how could he know? He was never around long enough to learn anything important.

She took off at a run for Stefan's house, her mind saying one minute that she should never have given in so easily, that Red would think he could get away with anything he wanted, and the next minute saying she'd made Melanie happy and that was all that counted.

Stefan was so excited he could hardly put his words together in a string. "But Mother's not here— Jeez, I don't—! She never lets me—"

"What about Lupe? You could ask her."

"It's not up to Lupe. If my dad was here, he'd talk Mother into it. Maybe."

Carolina watched Stefan caught between obeying his mother and his own mounting excitement. Stuck in the middle, just as she had been. "I'll leave her a note," he decided at last, his mouth in a straight, grim line. "It'll be too late by the time she sees it. We'll be charging across the high seas!"

Carolina helped Stefan find a warm sweater, his plaid scarf, and a windbreaker. Then they were off down the hall, two fugitives heading for the elevator and freedom. Racing across the bumpy field, she nearly dumped him twice, but Stefan hung on, urging Carolina to push harder, run faster. Then he took over the job himself, leaning forward, his palms slapping the wheels while Carolina ran alongside. Crow, caught up in the excitement, hopped from Carolina's shoulder to Stefan's curved back, catching Stefan's wind under his wings.

The *Mary Louise* was berthed in a line of boats that looked more or less alike, white boats with blue or black trim, boats shaped like giant bathtubs with worn wooden decks. She was an old girl, Red had told them when he first bought the boat, patting her deck rail as if she could hear him.

He would change her name to Melanie, he said, but he never had.

There were seagulls everywhere, staring down from the pulpit, strutting the deck as if they owned this boat and all the others, too. Red flapped his arms at them and they lifted straight up, their wings and legs extended, but only one flew off.

Crow stomped nervously on Carolina's shoulder. Then he leaped up on her head, the place he went when he needed to get a real good look at things. From deep within his chest came the strange sound he'd made when he first met Frank the Ferret.

Red lifted Stefan, chair and all, onto the deck. Then he

reached for Trinity, stowed her neatly under his arm, and stuck a hand out for Melanie. Carolina hopped on without his help. She reminded herself that she didn't *have* to talk to Red. He couldn't *make* her look at him. But the more she tried not to look at him, the more she had to think about it.

It was enough to make a person crazy.

Red hauled out the orange life vests and helped Stefan strap his on. Melanie smeared sunscreen on Stefan's pale face, then on Trinity and Carolina as well. All the while Stefan asked Red questions: Had Red ever seen a whale? (Red had, hundreds of them.) Had he ever gone down in a boat? (He hadn't, and hoped he never would.) Was the *Mary Louise* really fast? (She was a "real dog," Red said, but a fishing boat didn't have to be fast. It just had to get you where you were going, out to where the fish were. Or were not.)

When his passengers were settled, Red started up the big engines. They rumbled underfoot, the water churning white from the big propeller, and the *Mary Louise* began chugging out of the harbor toward the open sea.

"Jeez!" cried Stefan as the palm-lined streets grew tiny in the distance. "Wow! I can't believe I'm on a boat! Jeez!" His pale thin face had color for the first time, and his blue eyes sparkled with excitement. Trinity fell right to sleep, the way she always did on the boat, as if it were the world's safest place to be.

Carolina scrambled up to the bow, Melanie's warnings to

be careful carried off by the wind. But she was always careful, Red knew that. He trusted her with the run of the boat. He even let her steer if she wanted to.

How could somebody be good and bad all at the same time? It wasn't like in the movies or in books. People could be more than one thing. And that, too, was enough to make a person crazy.

Ahead, like giant gray whales floating on the surface of the sea, were the Channel Islands. Red said they'd go around the back side of Santa Cruz, the nearest one, and anchor there for lunch. The wind blew Carolina's eyes almost closed and tossed her hair in all directions as the *Mary Louise* plowed ahead. Crow's claws dug into her shoulder. Pulling his head down into his body, he scooted into the hollow of her neck and hung on, eyes shut, his feathers ruffling.

And then they came, just as she'd hoped, skimming along the bow on both sides, silvery shapes just below the surface. "Dolphins!" she yelled, and Red gave the thumbs-up sign. She'd seen them only once before, but Red said he saw them all the time. They liked to play with boats, he'd told her, racing along with the fastest of them, crisscrossing back and forth under the bow. As Carolina watched, stretched full-length on her stomach, a dolphin leaped straight up, then curved into a clean dive to re-enter the churning water. "Crow! Look at that!" Carolina yelled. Crow had climbed to the top of her head again and peered down into the water, his claws holding fast to her hair.

And then they disappeared, quicker than the eye could know it, as fast as they'd come.

Carolina scrambled back to the deck. Stefan was, for once, speechless. His mouth hung open, as if the wind had snatched away all the perfect words.

"Cool, huh?" said Carolina.

Stefan nodded, his eyes wide. "Cool," he breathed.

They anchored inside a calm cove on the back side of the island and ate their lunch. "I could live here," Stefan said, his mouth full of peanut butter and jelly. "I'm going to be a naturalist someday," he told Red in the serious-old-man way he had. "A famous naturalist. It's important that I have experiences like this."

Red agreed, looking as serious as Red could be. "Ever been to sea before?"

"Nope."

"And you were born right here? In Santa Barbara?"

"Yes, sir," said Stefan. "But my dad gets seasick and my mom, well, she doesn't think I can . . . She doesn't let me do much." Stefan frowned at his half-eaten sandwich, and Carolina could tell he was thinking about all the time he spent in his room instead of out in the world where a someday-naturalist was meant to be.

"Well, you're welcome to come along with me," Red said. "I can always use the company."

Stefan gulped. "You mean it?"

"Sure!" said Red. "As long as the weather's good. There's things you can do on the boat, you know, to help me out."

"Wow!" Stefan said. "Thanks!"

Carolina pinched her lips closed to keep from telling Stefan the truth. That he shouldn't count on Red. That nobody could. But why ruin it for him? Maybe Red *would* take him out sometime, like he said. She didn't know for sure that he wouldn't.

The *Mary Louise* rocked gently beneath them as Melanie cut the carrot cake. Trinity toddled around the deck like a drunken sailor, falling and picking herself up again. Crow hopped back and forth with a piece of fishing lure dangling from his beak. Red stretched his long legs halfway across the deck. "That bird ever gonna fly?"

"When he wants to," Carolina said to the deck.

"And when's that?"

"Ask *him*," said Carolina. "He knows."

On the way back, Red hoisted Stefan onto his big shoulders so that Stefan could look for whales. It was late in the season, Red said. Most of them were already in Mexico. But Stefan saw spouts everywhere, just the same. As they pulled into the harbor, the sky was scudding over and Red predicted rain.

# 11

Carolina began teaching Crow how to fly. Not near the cliff where Melanie would have tossed him, but out in the open field where Crow could look up and see birds just like him crossing the sky.

If Red came by, Melanie said that morning, he'd have some good news. Carolina guessed what it was and didn't want to hear it. And she didn't want to see Red. He forgot too easily. He tried to make everything better by laughing or whistling or offering boat rides.

Carolina set Crow on the top of her hand. "Okay, ready?"

Crow blinked and ducked under his wing for a mite.

"Here we go!" cried Carolina, taking off across the field as fast as she could run. Crow bounced along on her hand, his feathers ruffling in the slight breeze Carolina made. "Okay, now fly!" she yelled, and tried to shake him off her hand. But the harder she shook, the tighter he clung. She stopped at last, breathless. "Oh, Crow!" she cried. "How are you ever going to learn if you don't even try?"

Crow cocked his head.

"Don't you want to fly?"

He hopped onto her shoulder.

"Dumb bird," she muttered.

She found a flat rock and sat down to rest. She could run back and forth across the field all morning and Crow would just think they were playing games.

From where she sat the yellow bus looked very small, like a child's toy. She looked at it for the first time the way somebody else would, somebody who didn't love the bus. She looked at it the way the young policeman had. But then she felt very sad and very far away from Melanie, so she stretched out on the warm flat rock and closed her eyes. The sun made her feel sleepy and safe, as if she had no problems, only dreams. She pictured the house with the blue door that she would someday buy for Melanie. She took Melanie's hand and they walked through all the beautiful rooms. Behind the house she put the old school bus that they would drive around in sometimes, but only for fun.

She tried not to think about how it would be to live with the Crouches. That seemed far away, too, another kind of dream.

She got up, expecting to find Crow nearby. She turned in a circle. She turned again, the other way. She called him, her hand cupped over her forehead to shade her eyes. Her heart began to pound. "Crow!" she cried. In all directions the field with its mashed-down weeds stretched empty. "Crow!" Calling for him, Carolina ran toward the soldier trees. Maybe after all this time he'd remembered something. Remembered his mother, remembered falling. "Crow!"

Why didn't he have a name? What seemed to make sense before suddenly seemed stupid and heartless.

In the shade of the great trees only the leaves spoke, and then, high above, a single piercing caw. Carolina peered up. Could it be Crow? Could he have gotten himself into the trees when he couldn't fly? Had he been pretending all along? Was he the lazy little hitchhiker Melanie said he was?

Standing with her fists on her hipbones, staring up into the trees, Carolina felt the tears start up. Upset with herself, she brushed them away. She'd wanted him to fly, didn't she? She wanted him to be free. So what was she crying about?

She waited longer than she'd waited for Crow's mother that dark morning when she'd first heard a cry and found him, a pimpled, white, featherless lump. She thought about the way one day or one person or even one bird could change your whole life forever.

At last she turned away. "Goodbye, Crow," she said, just in case he could hear her. "I love you!" Her words echoed through the soldier trees, sounding strange to her even now when it was too late. She'd never given Crow a name and she'd never told him how much she loved him. Now she wondered why. Was it because he was a bird? But how dumb was that? If she loved him, she should have told him so.

She scuffed her way back across the field toward the bus, to Melanie, her head hanging. Tears flowed and dripped off her chin. When she heard Melanie calling her name, she looked up. And there was Crow, a black speck at Melanie's feet. She took off running, the wings of her heart lifting.

"Where were you?" Melanie asked. Trinity sat on her blanket chewing on her red sun hat. "When Crow showed up without you, I started to worry! I was just about to grab Trinity and go searching."

Carolina set her hand on the ground and Crow scurried up her arm. "Dumb bird," she said, but she'd have hugged him if she could. If she wouldn't crush him.

"You just missed Red," said Melanie.

"Too bad," said Carolina sourly. "What's the good news?"

Melanie frowned. "Well," she said, "you may not think it's so good . . ."

"Then it's bad."

"Co!" cried Trinity, and made a grab for Crow's tail.

"Not for Red and, honey, not for us either," Melanie said. "Red got a job, a *real* job."

"Fishing's a job!"

"Of course it is, but this one is, well, more steady. He's going to work in a fishery."

"In Oregon, right?"

"Well, I told you that . . ."

"I know," said Carolina, her throat thick with tears.

"He wants us to go with him, honey."

Carolina had known what Melanie would say, because she'd heard the words before. She turned away, but Melanie grabbed her shoulders, drawing her back. "It's the best thing," Melanie said. "It's our chance to have a house, Caro. That little house we've always talked about . . ."

"And Red."

Melanie sighed. "He loves us, honey. He really does."

Carolina pulled away from Melanie. "I'm not going," she said to the ground. She looked around for Crow and saw him scurrying off with a pop-top to his hiding place. "*We're* not going."

"*Sweet*heart!"

"I mean it, Melanie. Crow can't go to Oregon. He lives right here." Carolina plunked down on the bottom step of the bus. "And so do we."

Melanie squeezed in beside Carolina. "I have to go, Caro. I can't find a job here. We've used all the food stamps and we're almost out of money."

"You *could* get a job," Carolina muttered. "You got one before. You didn't look hard enough. You never wanted to stay!"

"That's not fair, Carolina. You know how hard I've tried."

"But only until Red came back. You just want to live with him. You don't care about us!" Carolina stumbled up the steps, ran to her bed, and threw herself facedown.

She awoke with the afternoon sun beaming down on

her face and Crow on her chest. She sat up and looked around her "room."

There wasn't much to pack. She could take it all in one trip.

On Melanie's bed was a note: *Went to the store. Back soon. I love you.*

Carolina began stuffing her backpack with T-shirts.

Melanie had scraped enough change together to buy macaroni and cheese, Carolina's favorite box dinner. She lit the camp stove and set a pan of water over the flames. Then she rinsed some lettuce leaves in the washbowl and dried them with a paper towel. "Feeling better?"

Melanie was wearing the black dress, which meant that Red was probably coming back.

Carolina shrugged.

"You remember how beautiful Oregon is, don't you? All those big trees! I felt so free in Oregon, didn't you?" In the candlelight, Melanie's dangling gold-plated earrings looked almost real.

"I'm not going with you," Carolina announced, her voice wobbling. "I've decided to go to the Crouches'."

Melanie dropped the lettuce into the washbowl, splattering the front of her dress with water. "Honey, *no!*"

"You said I get to make all the big decisions."

"Well, yes, I know. But—"

"But what? Is it my decision or isn't it?"

Candlelight cast shadows over Melanie's face. She looked as if she was about to cry. "Caro, you just can't . . .

can't go live with somebody else. Why would you want to do that?"

It felt wrong to frighten Melanie, but she did it anyway. "Is it or isn't it?"

Melanie placed her fingers over her lips and looked through wide worried eyes at her daughter. Then she dropped her hand to her lap. "Yes," she said at last. "Yes, I guess it is your decision. I mean, I *did* say you could make the big decisions, but—"

"Okay, then," said Carolina. "Then I'm going."

Melanie started to say something. Then she just stared at Carolina as if her daughter had turned into somebody else. "Well!" she said at last, biting her lip. "Well, you *can't* go. I've changed my mind. I won't let you."

"But you said . . . !"

Impatiently Melanie waved away what had come before. "I don't care what I said. It was dumb, what I said. You're my daughter and you can't just go live with . . . with strangers."

Melanie was crying now, and so was Carolina. But Carolina's tears were angry ones. Melanie couldn't have it her way, not this time.

"Then tell Red we're not going to Oregon. Tell him we're staying right here."

Melanie grabbed the roll of toilet paper and blew her nose. "I can't, honey. I can't do that."

"Then I'm going to the Crouches'," Carolina said, her voice strong and hard, "and you can't stop me!"

"Sweetheart . . ." Melanie began. Then she leaned forward and clutched Carolina's wrist. There was fear in her eyes. She began to sound desperate. "Look, honey," she pleaded. Her hand on Carolina's wrist felt cold. "I have an idea. How about if we ask the Crouches if you can stay for a week. How would that be? While Red . . . while we get settled. School doesn't start for a couple of weeks."

*I'll never live with Red,* thought Carolina, but she could see that Melanie wasn't going to let her go. "Two weeks," she insisted, just to have her way.

Melanie frowned. At last she gave in. "All right, two weeks. If it's okay with the Crouches."

It wasn't hard to lie to Melanie when it was for her own good. She'd find out how easy it was to have just one kid— the way it used to be when it was just the two of them, her and Melanie. Then Carolina would tell her the truth: she was going to live with the Crouches forever. Melanie could have her crazy life of freedom on the road. She could have Red. Maybe he'd stick around longer if Carolina wasn't there.

Melanie seemed lighter now that they'd settled things. "In a couple of weeks Crow might be flying," she said, "and you'll feel better about leaving him."

"Maybe," said Carolina. The macaroni and cheese tasted like paper and glue. Carolina could barely swallow it. Trinity smeared her face with the orangy-yellow sauce and nobody laughed.

Melanie wet a washrag and attacked Trinity's face. "We'll have to ask the Crouches tomorrow."

Carolina's heart fell. "Are you leaving so soon?"

"Thursday. Red's job starts next week."

"Red!" Carolina cried, her face hot and the tears starting up again. "It's *always* Red. What about *us*, huh? What about Trinity and me? What about what *we* want?"

"Honey . . . !" But Carolina twisted out of Melanie's reach and pushed out through the door of the bus, so fast Crow was left behind. She took off across the field at a run, her heart hammering. *I don't care, I don't care, I don't care. Let her have Red. I don't care.*

And then it was Thursday. Carolina had little to pack, so it took no time at all to get ready. Melanie's eyes were puffy and red. Her curls were sprung in all directions. She hadn't slept a wink, she said. They'd never been apart before. Two weeks was a long time, fourteen days. Was Carolina sure this was what she wanted to do?

Carolina picked up Trinity and hugged her hard. "Goodbye, little mugger," she said, biting back tears. Trinity wriggled to get down, but Carolina set her in her pack, which Melanie had already strapped on.

"Here, I can carry something," said Melanie. Carolina passed her the sleeping bag.

"Why are you taking this?"

Carolina shrugged. "I don't know. I just want it." She slid into her backpack and grabbed Crow's basket. "C'mon, Crow."

They set off across the field in a gray morning drizzle that was almost rain. Melanie was nervous, but Carolina wasn't going to worry about her. Not anymore. She had

Red to do that now. "You have the number, right?" Melanie said for the third time. If Carolina needed to reach Melanie, she could call Red's workplace and leave a message. Then Melanie would telephone her back. "I'll call you on Wednesday, okay? Nine o'clock, right?"

"Yes," said Carolina.

"Are you absolutely *sure* this is what you want to do?" Melanie's curls collected tiny silver raindrops. Trinity wore her red hat, which was meant for sunny days.

Carolina didn't answer. Melanie had asked the same question a dozen times and she'd always said that, yes, this was exactly what she wanted to do. There was something cold and hard as stone where her heart once was, and she worked to keep it there.

The big door swung open and there stood a round little man with Stefan's pale face and a pointed white beard. His eyebrows rose as Melanie introduced herself and Carolina. "I'm Stefan Crouch," he said in a deep, gruff voice, extending his hand to both of them in turn. "Madeleine told me you were coming to stay for a little while, Carolina. Won't you both—ah, won't you *all* come in?"

He didn't really look mean, just serious or worried. Anyway, he didn't look like he could swallow children. "Madeleine told me all about you, Carolina." He turned to Lupe, who had come up quietly behind him. "Would you call the Missus, Lupe? And Stefan! He's been so excited." He smiled for the first time and looked quickly away. Mr. Crouch wasn't mean, he was shy! Carolina wondered how it was possible that a grown-up man, a rich grown-up man, could be shy. Some of the fear that she'd carried across the field began to leave her.

"Will you give us just a minute?" said Melanie in a near-whisper.

"Of course, my dear!" said Mr. Crouch, turning to leave, his forehead creased with concern. "Don't worry, we'll take good care of your girl and you'll have her back in no time!" Carolina hoped he'd be just as cheerful when he learned she was ready to stay forever.

Wordlessly, Melanie folded Carolina in her arms and began to rock her gently back and forth as if she were a baby once again, a baby who'd awakened from a bad dream in the middle of the night. Her wet curls tickled Carolina's nose. When she finally let Carolina go, Melanie's face was wet and her eyes were red. She shook her head as if she couldn't believe what was happening. "I don't know what's the matter with me! You're eleven years old. Old enough to stay with a friend for a couple of weeks. It's like camp or something!"

Carolina opened her mouth to say goodbye, but nothing came out. Not a whisper, not a squeak. Nothing.

She blinked once, and her mother was gone into the mist. Only Trinity's red hat bobbed in the distance, and then that, too, disappeared.

# 12

"I can't tell you how happy you've made me, made *us*!" said Mrs. Crouch. "Come, we'll get you settled." With her sleeping bag under one arm, backpack on her back, and Crow on her shoulder, Carolina followed Stefan's mother down the hall. At the door to Heather's room, Mrs. Crouch took the key on the ribbon from around her neck and fit it into the lock. The door swung open, but this time, instead of the fluffy white rug and the great white bed, what Carolina saw immediately was the cage. It was a big black wire contraption with a domed top, and it hung from an iron ring on a very tall stand. Crow dug his claws into Carolina's shoulder.

Carolina looked up at Mrs. Crouch. "Is that for Crow?" Her voice came out as a rusty squeak.

"Yes!" Stefan's mother crossed the room and opened the

door to the cage. "It's the biggest one we could find. I'm sure he'll do just fine in here."

"But Crow's never been in a cage!"

"It's just for when you're in the house," Mrs. Crouch explained. "We can't have birds and animals running all over the place, now, can we?" Then she began explaining other things. About the way the lights dimmed with a little turn of a switch and how Carolina could adjust the thermostat. There were extra blankets in the white chest at the end of the bed. But Carolina hardly heard. Her eyes kept going to the awful cage. She couldn't disobey Stefan's mother, especially not if she was going to ask to stay forever. But she would never put Crow in a cage. She would never take away his freedom.

"Well!" said Mrs. Crouch. She reached down to smooth Carolina's wild hair, then drew her hand back. "You'll want to get dressed for dinner. Why don't I just leave you alone to get settled." And she was gone, trusting Carolina to do what she said. To put Crow in the cage.

A knock on the door, and there was Stefan. "Your very own mice," he said, handing her a small silver cage. "For company." Carolina didn't know whether to laugh or cry.

"Your mother said I should dress for dinner. And that *cage*, Stefan!" She pointed at the ugly black monstrosity hanging from its stand. "It's for Crow."

"Oh, yeah. I told her not to buy it, but she wouldn't listen." He held up his hand, and Crow hopped on. "Don't worry about it. Crow doesn't have to stay in there. She won't know the difference."

"But—"

"If you're worried about what to wear, just wear Heather's stuff. Mother expects you to." He handed Crow back to Carolina and wheeled toward the door, then turned back. "Mother said to make you feel welcome. So I brought you the mice, but . . . Hey! It's great you're here, you know?" Then he, too, was gone.

With Crow still on her shoulder, Carolina went into Heather's closet and found the velvet dress. She laid it carefully on the big white bed. Then she left Heather's room, closing the door quietly behind her. She took Crow's basket with her.

The sun was going down behind the soldier trees, melting in a golden pool on the surface of the dark water. She found a pine tree not far from the house with branches that dipped nearly to the ground and settled Crow's basket inside. Then she put Crow into his basket. He cocked his head as if to say, "It's not my bedtime." But he stayed in the basket, and when she turned at the big front door, she could see that he was still there.

Halfway down the hall to Heather's room, Carolina almost turned back. What had she done? Crow wouldn't be safe outside without her. He'd never been alone for very long. He could get used to the cage. He'd only be in it at night. That way he'd be safe.

But when she opened the door and saw the big ugly black prison waiting, she knew she couldn't do it to him.

Carolina took off her jeans and T-shirt, folded them, and put them in a dresser drawer that Mrs. Crouch said was for her things. The velvet dress slid over her head and down over her body. It was heavier than she thought it would be, but it fit like a dress was supposed to. She looked at herself in the closet mirror and knew she'd have to comb the knots out of her hair. She thought about Melanie and how they fought about hair combing and was sorry she'd been so awful. And she wondered if Stefan's mother had combed Heather's hair or giggled with her in the big white bed or danced around a school bus. She missed Melanie so much it almost hurt to breathe.

Mr. and Mrs. Crouch and Stefan were waiting at the long dining-room table. She wondered how long they'd been sitting there and whether they'd heard her leave the house on her way to dinner to check on Crow again. "How nice you look, dear!" said Mrs. Crouch at one end of the long table, but Carolina could see from her expression that she'd worn the wrong thing. Velvet was probably just for very special occasions. Maybe this *was* a special occasion, her first night here. After all, there were candles on the table. But if it was special, it sure didn't feel that way.

Stefan's father slid back her chair, and Carolina sat down across the table from Stefan.

"I asked Lupe to make chicken," said Stefan. "Your favorite. And for dessert there's—"

"Oh!" cried Stefan's mother, her hand on her heart. "Chicken was Heather's favorite, too! Isn't that odd?"

Lupe came out and filled their water glasses. Then she

served salads that had been put on little plates. Each plate had one piece of lettuce, two slices of tomato, and a slice of avocado in a frown. Carolina was careful to do exactly what Stefan did. When he smoothed his cloth napkin over his lap, she did the same. When he picked up the small fork, so did she.

"Well, I propose a toast!" said Stefan's father. "To our houseguest, Carolina." His round face looked dark red in the candlelight and his eyes twinkled.

"And to her dear, brave mother," added Mrs. Crouch.

"Hear! Hear!" said Stefan, raising his water glass.

"Some families we know don't sit down to dinner together," said Mrs. Crouch, leaning her tall body toward Carolina as if she were telling her a secret, "but we always do. We share what happened in our day. Don't we, Stefan?"

"Yes, we do," said Stefan. Frowning to keep from laughing, he said in a robot's voice, "We share what happened in our day."

"Why don't you start, darling," said Mrs. Crouch to her husband.

He cleared his throat and began to talk about someone called Mr. Tweedle, who lived in London, and something called a merger. Stefan rolled his eyes at Carolina. When Mr. Crouch was finished, Mrs. Crouch went on and on about the rummage sale, where they'd sold every one of the dresses to help the battered women. When Stefan's turn came, Carolina could see he'd been waiting. "Well," he said, just as Lupe came out with the dinner plates, "first

I cleaned the mouse cage. Whew! Did it ever stink. The newspaper was sopping wet with pee and—"

"That's enough, Stefan," said both his father and mother at the same time.

"But you wanted to know about my day. I was sharing!"

Nervous giggles rose in Carolina's throat, but she swallowed them.

Lupe took away the salad plates. Then she served them each a plate with a tiny cooked bird in the middle. On one side of the bird were six of the skinniest string beans Carolina had ever seen. On the other was a spoonful of mashed potatoes.

*"Bon appétit!"* called Mr. Crouch from his end of the table.

"See? We speak French at dinner, too," said Stefan. "But we *share* in English."

"Stefan, you're being obnoxious," said his mother. "Carolina hasn't had her chance to share—" She cut herself off, but not in time for them all to think about the kind of day Carolina had had saying goodbye to her mother and baby sister.

"There will be plenty of chances for Carolina to share," said Mr. Crouch smoothly. "If she wants to. She's our guest, after all. Only members of the family have to share. Isn't that right, my dear?"

"Oh, but she seems like a member of the family already." She turned to her husband. "Doesn't she, dear? Doesn't she, Stefan?" She turned to her son.

"Certainly," agreed Mr. Crouch.

"Certainly!" cried Stefan, mimicking his father.

Carolina couldn't wait for the dinner to end. She'd been watching the window behind Stefan's head growing darker and darker. At last Mrs. Crouch rang her little bell and told Lupe that she and Mr. Crouch would retire to the library for their brandy. Carolina bolted from her chair.

"Carolina?"

"Yes, ma'am?"

"You forgot to excuse yourself."

Carolina felt her face grow hot. "I'm sorry," she said. "Excuse me, okay?"

"May I please be excused," instructed Mrs. Crouch, with a lift of her chin.

"May I please be excused," repeated Carolina.

"You may," said Mrs. Crouch, and Carolina took off for the front door.

Stefan excused himself and scooted right after her. "Where are you going?"

"Out to check on Crow." It took all her strength to pull the great door open.

"Crow's outside?"

"I can't put him in that cage, Stefan," Carolina said miserably. "I just can't."

"But he'd be safe—"

"I know! I know he would." She headed for the pine tree. "But he'd hate it. I have to think about what *he* wants."

"But aren't you scared something will happen to him?"

Carolina knelt down and saw that Crow was sleeping,

his head tucked under his wing. "Of course, silly," she whispered. "What do you think?"

Back in the house Stefan named a dozen things they could do. Halfway through a game of Parcheesi Carolina yawned, pretending to be sleepy. "Guess I'll go to bed," she said.

"Oh, okay . . ." said Stefan, clearly disappointed. But Carolina didn't think she should tell him what she planned to do and make him her accomplice. She could get him in trouble, and the Crouches would never let her stay.

In Heather's room she changed out of the black velvet dress into one of Heather's flannel nightgowns. She grabbed her sleeping bag and flip-flops. Then she went very quietly down the long, dark hallway in her bare feet.

A warm wind was blowing the tops of the trees around. It lifted her hair and the hem of Heather's nightgown. At the pine tree she knelt and peered inside the branches. Crow's basket was empty. "Crow!" she cried in a loud whisper. "Crow, where are you?"

He came hopping up and stood beside her. Weak with relief, she leaned down and gave him her arm to scurry up.

They crossed the field against the wind. Overhead were a scattering of the zillion stars she'd seen through the bus window the night Crow called to her. Walking through the dark field was like drifting through those stars.

Somewhere between the mansion and the clump of trees that had almost hidden their bus, Carolina stopped. The wind teased her hair and lifted Crow's feathers. It dried the tears that came into her eyes. She stood that way, looking across the field for the longest time, making her eyes believe what her mind had known all along: Melanie wouldn't be there. There was nothing as empty as empty was. Like a hole in the heart. The bus was gone.

# 13

She opened her eyes to silver spokes. "What are you doing out here?" Stefan leaned over the arm of his chair, staring down with puzzled blue eyes.

Carolina rubbed her face and stretched. Crow stood up in his basket, ruffling his wings. Then she remembered where she was and why. "Don't tell, okay? Please?" In a patch of soft ground beneath the pine tree where the needles lay thick, she had slept straight through the night.

"Well, okay, cool," said Stefan uncertainly. "But are you going to sleep out here all the time?"

"I guess," she said. They both looked at Crow, who was pecking at a snail shell.

"Let's do something," said Stefan.

"What?" Carolina got up, brushing pine needles off Heather's nightgown and out of her hair.

"I dunno. Wanna go to the zoo?"

"Uh-uh," said Carolina, rolling up her sleeping bag. "The zoo makes me sad. Let's go to the harbor."

"Sometimes animals have to be in cages, Carolina," said Stefan in his lecture voice. "It's for their own good. To protect them."

"Not Frank," she said. "Frank doesn't need to be in a cage."

"Okay, okay," he said. "I'll let Frank go. Jeez! *Then* we'll go somewhere, okay?"

They went into the house. Carolina changed clothes while Stefan went off to fetch Frank's cage. They met outside. "Over there." Stefan pointed to a thick stand of bushes and low trees.

When Stefan found the exact right spot, Carolina set Frank's cage on the ground and opened the door. The ferret stuck his nose halfway out, glanced quickly around with his beady dark eyes, and shot off into the bushes.

They spent the day exploring, Carolina pushing Stefan's chair because it was fun and because he let her. Carolina was amazed at how little Stefan knew about his own city, the city he'd been born and raised in. They window-shopped on State Street. They bumped down the rough planks of Stearns Wharf and watched the old men fishing while huge brown pelicans stomped back and forth in search of free fish. "There's Santa Cruz," said Stefan, pointing at the island. "I wonder if Red will ever come back. Do you think he will?"

Carolina didn't want to crush Stefan's hopes. "He could," she said. "You never know with Red."

"I wish the *Mary Louise* was here," said Stefan. "I'd like to see her just one more time."

They went to the marina anyway to look at all the other boats, and there, right where she wasn't supposed to be, was the *Mary Louise.*

"Maybe he's leaving today," Stefan suggested.

"But he was supposed to leave on Wednesday." Carolina jumped onto the *Mary Louise*'s deck. Her ropes and nets were stowed neatly in milk crates, her hatch double-padlocked.

Stefan peered up at Carolina, his mind churning. "Maybe the engine broke down or something."

They went up and down the marina looking for Red and asking other fishermen if they had seen him. No one had.

"Maybe he took the bus instead," said Stefan, still searching for reasons why Red wasn't already in Oregon with Melanie. "Or hitchhiked or something."

"Maybe," said Carolina.

Maybe not, she thought.


Stefan bought double-decker ice-cream cones for their lunch.

By the time they returned to the mansion, the sun was setting in bands of orange, gold, and blue the color of Stefan's eyes.

"Where in the world have you two been?" Mrs. Crouch's

hair had sprung loose from her bun. She stood in the doorway blocking their entrance, demanding an explanation.

Stefan, who had laughed and talked a hundred miles an hour all day, suddenly lost his voice.

Carolina spoke up. "It's my fault," she said. "I didn't know what time it was. We just went downtown and to the harbor . . ."

"The idea!" cried Mrs. Crouch. "You look like a couple of ragamuffins! Get in the house this minute!"

Carolina fled to her room—Heather's room—while Stefan's mother continued to lecture her son, her angry words echoing down the hall. "You did *not* have permission . . . Whatever gave you the idea you could just *leave* this house whenever you wanted . . . Your health is delicate. You can't just run around like a stray dog—"

Carolina closed the door on whatever came next. Stefan's mother wanted Stefan to be "delicate," but he wasn't delicate. She kept him in a cage the way Stefan had kept Frank, and it just wasn't right.

Remembering how fast Frank took off after his cage door was opened and he got a sniff of the open air made Carolina smile. Stefan had looked just the same as they'd headed downtown.


"I was thinking, Carolina," said Stefan's mother at dinner the next night.

"Uh-oh," muttered Stefan.

*"Stefan,"* warned his father.

"While you're here you might want to take a few

lessons." There were tall candlesticks all down the length of the table. Mrs. Crouch's long, sad-looking face wavered in the candlelight.

Stefan's father smiled genially. "Right!" he said. "It's never too soon to start, you know." Then he looked quickly at his apple-crumb dessert as if it demanded all his attention.

"Lessons?" said Carolina.

"Yes. You know . . . ballet, gymnastics, piano. Whatever you'd like. I think that you and Stefan have far too much free time on your hands." She rang a little bell and Lupe popped through the door. "We're finished, Lupe," she said.

Carolina thought about lessons while Lupe cleared the table. "I'd like to learn to fish," she said at last. "Are there fishing lessons?"

Stefan's father let out a guffaw. "That's rich!" he said.

Mrs. Crouch shot him a look.

"How about ballet?" she said. "You can always tell when a woman has been trained in dance." She sat straighter in her chair, pulling back her shoulders.

"I don't think so," said Carolina. "But thank you just the same."

"Piano, then?"

She clasped her stubby brown fingers together. "No, thank you."

Mrs. Crouch frowned down the length of the table. "There must be *something*," she said, "besides *fishing*, that you'd like."

"Give her a chance, Madeleine," Stefan's father said.

"The child just got here. She's on vacation, for heaven's sake. She doesn't need lessons."

Mrs. Crouch was quiet for several minutes, thinking. "But she could use some clothes," she said at last. "All little girls love clothes, don't they, Carolina?"

Carolina, knowing she was supposed to love clothes more than she did, nodded politely.

"Well!" cried Mrs. Crouch, clapping her hands. "We'll go shopping. We'll get hair trims and manicures and then we'll have lunch. Just like mothers and . . ." She blinked several times, her eyes shiny and wet. "Oh, we're going to have such fun!"

They went shopping the very next afternoon. While they wandered the perfumed aisles of glistening department stores, Stefan waited outside with Crow on his head. "I think it's time for this bird to fly," he said grimly. And it was. Stefan had told Carolina that Crow's tail had grown long enough. He said that he couldn't understand why the bird wasn't flying yet. He thought maybe Crow was having too much fun with them.

Carolina did her best to act as excited as Stefan's mother was about all the clothes she bought—dresses, pleated skirts, matching sweater sets, dress shoes and play shoes, underwear, socks with tiny bows. All Carolina wanted was a pair of new jeans that she could start breaking in before school started, but Mrs. Crouch said almost exactly what Melanie had said about jeans. They just weren't "appropriate" for sixth grade.

On the way home they passed Stefan's school. It looked like a fancy house with a tall iron gate. COUNTRY DAY SCHOOL said a brass plaque attached to the gate. There were no swing sets, no monkey bars. "Shush," it seemed to say. "Shush."

On Wednesday morning Carolina waited by Heather's Princess telephone for Melanie to call. The pink phone rang at ten to nine and Carolina snatched it up. "Mom?"

"I couldn't wait another minute!" cried Melanie. "How are you, honey? Are you all right? Are you having fun?" Carolina could hear traffic in the background.

"Sure, I guess," said Carolina. "Where are you?"

"Winchester Bay," said Melanie. "Near the fishery. It's pretty foggy here, but I can see it's a nice little town. I haven't heard from Red yet, but I'm sure he's on his way."

Carolina knew she had to tell Melanie sooner or later. "The boat's still here, Melanie," she said, and bit her lip.

Silence. The sound of traffic.

"I saw her, the *Mary Louise*."

"Oh."

"You haven't heard from him?"

"Not yet. Maybe something went wrong with the boat. That happens sometimes . . ."

"Yeah . . ."

"I'm sure he's coming . . ."

Melanie sounded very far away, farther than Oregon,

111

farther than the stars. "I miss you, Caro," she said. "Trinity won't eat. It might be a cold, but I think she's missing you. Two weeks is too long."

"I miss you, too," Carolina said over the lump in her throat. "You two, too!"

"But it's great, huh? Your room and all? I never did see it. You'll have to write to me, tell me all about it, okay? Draw me a picture."

"Sure."

A mechanical voice cut in, saying that more coins had to be deposited. "Shoot!" cried Melanie. "Wait! I've got some more change—"

"That's okay, Melanie. You shouldn't spend the money."

"Okay, swee—" The phone went dead.

She pictured her mother standing by the side of the road at a phone booth in the fog, Trinity in her pack. Then she realized that without her big sister, Trinity couldn't get into the pack in the first place.

So she revised her picture. Now Melanie stood by the side of the road at a phone booth in the fog with Trinity clinging like a monkey to her hip. She couldn't walk far that way. Trinity was big for her age and Melanie was tiny. Who would put Trinity in her pack now that Carolina wasn't around? She was surprised Melanie had made it all the way to Oregon without Carolina reading the maps and telling her which way to turn.

Melanie by the side of the road, in the fog. Alone.

So Carolina made one of her big decisions, the one about God and heaven. It was easy, much easier than she had ever thought. "Dear God," she said, clasping her hands together like the picture she'd seen over the "Now I Lay Me Down to Sleep" prayer in her children's poetry book. "Please take care of my mom and baby sister." And then she didn't know what else to say. If God did that, it would be enough. "Amen," she said.

# 14

Stefan scooted around the far side of the long green pool table, studied the balls that were left, and set up his shot. Carolina watched how still he became, like a cat stalking a mouse, and thought she'd never be very good at pool. She could never stay still, Melanie said. *Zap* went Stefan's "custom stick," and another striped ball dropped neatly into a pocket.

Carolina put some more blue chalk on the end of her stick. "Leave some balls for me to hit," she said.

"Don't worry." Stefan's forehead was creased in concentration. "I'm just hitting the striped ones."

"But they're the ones that go in!" The tall, narrow windows were splattered with raindrops.

Stefan laughed. "You want me to show you how the other ones go in?"

"Nope, that's okay."

Stefan came back to where Carolina stood, took aim, and fired again. "Left corner pocket," he said, setting up for the orange-and-white ball, which headed straight where he wanted it to go. Crow hopped off Carolina's shoulder and ran across the table. Hunching over, he stared into the pocket where the ball had disappeared. "Wanna play again?"

"Maybe later," she said.

"But it's fun, huh? Isn't it?"

Stefan had everything a kid could ever want, Nintendo, computer games, books and paint sets and tons of paper, but no friends. At least none that Carolina knew about. And he never left the house.

"Well, not as much fun as going out to sea," he said. "You're so lucky!"

Lucky? That she lived in a school bus? That she didn't have a father? That they were poor? But what could she say to Stefan, who had no friends? Who couldn't run across a field? "Can I ask you something?"

"Sure."

"Did you always . . . I mean, were you always in that chair?"

"Well, I wasn't born in it, if that's what you mean." He laughed. "But almost, I guess. It's my spinal cord. It just didn't come together right."

"How come you don't have a new chair? One of the fancy ones with the buttons and all?"

Stefan patted the worn wooden arm of his chair. "I do have one of the fancy ones," he said. "I take it to school.

But this is my grandpa's old wheelchair," he said. "He was a cool guy. So am I. And so . . . ?" He hunched his shoulders, held out his palms, and laughed. So did Carolina. Stefan wheeled to the far end of the table with his stick. "Hey, there's our lunch."

Stefan scooted over to the door and held it open for Lupe, who came in carrying a big silver tray. She put it down and smoothed a white tablecloth on Mrs. Crouch's bridge table. Then she set the table with silver and folded linen napkins. Carolina noticed that on each fork, knife, and spoon there was a fancy-looking C. Real silver, too, it had to be. Then Lupe laid out the food, more sandwiches with cut-off crusts, only bigger this time. There were grapes with sugar stuck to them and bite-sized cookies inside crinkly paper cups. The last thing Lupe did was remove one of the chairs so that Stefan could roll himself up to the table. Carolina sat across from him, her skinned knees hidden beneath the skirt of the soft white tablecloth.

"Do you always eat like this?"

"Like what? Sandwiches and stuff? Sure."

"No, I mean this." She shrugged. *"Fancy."*

"Yeah." Stefan frowned. "It's kind of a drag, isn't it?"

"No, I didn't mean—"

"If it were up to me, I'd be eating on the deck of a boat. The *Mary Louise*! Except for my sixth birthday at Disneyland, that was the best day of my life so far. Red's great!"

"Yeah . . ." said Carolina, but her voice gave her away.

"Don't you like him? How come? I think he's cool." Stefan put a piece of bread on his palm and offered it to Crow. "How come he doesn't live with you on the bus? With your mom?"

Carolina shrugged. "I don't know. She wants him to marry her, but I guess he doesn't want to. So sometimes she won't let him stay all night, and then they fight about that . . ."

"Bummer," said Stefan.

"He's okay when he doesn't drink booze," she said.

"My parents have highballs," Stefan said. "That's a kind of drink. And they don't have just one either."

"But your father would never . . . never *hurt* your mom, would he?"

"Father? Heck no! He's a marshmallow. He just acts tough because he thinks he's supposed to."

Carolina tried to laugh along with Stefan, but her mind was full of big Red and little Melanie "dancing" in the moonlight. Now she wouldn't be there to stand between them. If Red pushed Melanie, or worse! she wouldn't even know.

Stefan popped a cookie in his mouth and pushed away from the table. "Okay, now I'll give you a lesson. It's no fun winning every time."

Carolina helped Stefan gather up the balls and watched him set them up in the wooden triangle. Then she pushed the triangle to where he wanted it. "I'll teach you how to break later," he said. "That's the hard part. Shoo, Crow!" Crow, who had perched himself in the middle of the lined-up balls, went back to Carolina's shoulder.

Stefan got very still over the white ball. *Crack* went his stick. Balls shot in all directions.

"I listened to Mom and Dad last night," said Stefan. "You know, through the grate. Dad's real loud and I can usually figure out what Mom's saying by hearing him." He took aim and shot his stick at the number 15. "Mother keeps talking like you're going to stay here forever. Dad keeps reminding her that it's only for two weeks."

It was time to let Stefan in on her secret. "What if," she said, biting her lip, "what if I did . . . stay?"

Stefan looked up in surprise, and number 15 went skidding off the rail. "You mean for good?"

"Yeah." Carolina chewed a piece of skin off the edge of her thumbnail.

"Well, yeah!" he said enthusiastically. "You know what I think. But are you sure that's what you want to do?"

Carolina shrugged. It was hard to look at Stefan and not tell the whole truth about how she really felt here in his house. "Sure," she said. "I mean, it could just be for school. I could go home for Christmas and stuff . . ."

"Yeah. And you can always call your mom on the phone and all . . ."


The next morning Carolina stood nervously in the doorway of Mrs. Crouch's sitting room. Mrs. Crouch was staring out the window while her hand stirred and stirred a cup of coffee. "Mrs. Crouch?"

Mrs. Crouch jumped. "Oh, Carolina! Won't you come

in, dear." She set her coffee cup down and laid the spoon in the saucer. "Is everything all right? Did you sleep well? You caught me daydreaming."

"I do that, too, sometimes."

"I'm sure you do," said Mrs. Crouch. "Come and sit," she said, and patted the place beside her on the flowery couch.

Carolina perched on the edge of a cushion at the far end. "I just wanted to ask something," she said. She pushed her hands between her knees. "Something about . . . about staying here."

"Yes?" She had every bit of Mrs. Crouch's attention and couldn't change her mind now.

"Would it be all right if I lived with you? I mean, not just for two weeks? For *real*?"

"Oh, Carolina! Of *course* it would. Nothing would please me more, nothing . . . But your mother! She's expecting you in Oregon."

"She'll let me stay," Carolina said quickly. "She lets me make my own decisions."

"Oh, I don't think she'd want . . . As much as I'd like . . ." Mrs. Crouch's fingers fluttered to her coffee cup, then up to the lace collar on her dress.

"It's up to me," insisted Carolina. "It *is*. It'll be easier for Melanie now. She won't need as much money, and maybe Red will stay, and well, it'll just be easier for her, that's all." She shrugged. On the edge of tears, she looked down at the two worn places on the knees of her jeans.

119

"Oh my dear," sighed Stefan's mother, forgetting her perfect posture as she slumped against the couch. "Easier," she said in a flat voice. "Whatever gave you that idea?" Carolina couldn't tell her she got it through the heater grate. "You're such a help to your mother."

"I know, but . . ."

"Having children, rearing a family . . . well, it isn't easy. Of course it isn't. It isn't meant to be." She looked at Carolina for the longest time with her sad dark eyes. "You must think long and hard about this decision, Carolina. I wish I could make it easier for you, but I cannot. I thought it would be better all around for you to come and live with us, and in some ways, it would be. You are a very special girl, as I've told your mother. You bring back into our lives some of the sunshine that we'd thought we'd lost forever. But"—she sighed—"I know I was only thinking of myself and how much I missed my darling Heather." She sighed deeply. "You mustn't make this decision for anyone but yourself, Carolina. Not for me, even though it may seem at times I want you to. Not for Stefan, not even for Melanie and your baby sister. Can you do that?" She reached out and touched Carolina's arm.

Carolina looked at the trembling fingers on her arm and could no longer hold back the tears. It was easier than she would have thought to be in Stefan's mother's arms. Just like Melanie, she knew how to make things all better, or when they couldn't be all better, at least to try.

# 15

Even though Mrs. Crouch had urged Carolina to make her own decision about where she would live, she carried right on with her daily plan to make Carolina feel "at home." A get-acquainted tea was "just the ticket," she said.

The girls began arriving at two o'clock on a dreary afternoon, their mothers dropping them off and whisking away again in shiny, low-slung cars and passenger vans. One girl, a tall redhead with braces, was delivered by a chauffeur in a white limousine.

Carolina stood nervously at Mrs. Crouch's side, wearing one of her new dresses. It itched around the neck where the lace was. Sweaty and uncomfortable, she practiced her lines in her head: My father is in the Spanish Air Force . . . They're holding my father for ransom in Libya . . . My mother sings opera in New York . . .

"Welcome! Welcome!" cried Mrs. Crouch as each girl

crossed the vestibule. "Stefan will take your things." Sweaters and jackets piled up on Stefan's lap.

"Just be yourself," Stefan said when Carolina told him how nervous she was about his mother's get-acquainted tea.

"You've got to be kidding!" she said. With a sweet, watery smile, Mrs. Crouch had presented Carolina with her first lip gloss—she'd never tell Melanie. It made her look like Raggedy Ann, so she rubbed it off on her wrist.

"Who are you going to be if you aren't yourself?" asked Stefan, genuinely puzzled.

Carolina had been staring in Heather's mirror at a girl with freshly washed, softly waved hair, wearing a green silk dress the color of her eyes.

"Who?" asked Stefan.

"*Who? Who?* You sound like an owl." She plunked down on Heather's bed and began picking the pink polish off her nails.

"Don't worry about the girls Mother invited. They're just, you know, *girls*. They'll be in your classes at Country Day, so you might as well get to know them. It's an *enriching* experience, Mother says."

"I wish we were out at sea," she said. "Running with the dolphins."

"So do I! Hey, maybe we can get somebody to take us out. One of those fishermen who hang out down there with nothing to do."

"Your mother would kill us," Carolina grumbled. "She

had a fit when you went out on Red's boat without asking."

"Yeah," said Stefan glumly. "That wasn't her idea of an enriching experience."

Now he sat by the doorway with lacy summer sweaters piled to his chin.

Mrs. Crouch ushered the girls into the living room that no one lived in. All the chairs and couches were arranged in circles. Heather gazed down from her spot over the fireplace. Carolina was supposed to go with Mrs. Crouch from circle to circle, so that all the girls would have a chance to meet her. If Melanie had thought of such a torture, Carolina would have talked her right out of it. But there was no reasoning with Mrs. Crouch, who appeared to be absolutely certain that she knew the right way to do everything.

She knew that Stefan's mother meant well, but this was worse than the worst first day of any school she'd ever been in.

"Linda Lee, Sondra, Jeanette Ellen," announced Mrs. Crouch in the first circle. "This is Carolina Lewis. She's staying with us for . . . for a while. I'm sure you'll all do your very best to make her feel welcome." And off she went.

Carolina swallowed hard and sat down.

Sondra's hair curled like pale golden wings on her shoulder blades. "Where are you from, Carolina? Did you just move here?" As she talked, her eyes swept slowly from the green ribbon in Carolina's hair down to her brand-new socks.

Carolina smoothed her dress over her scabby knees. "I was born in Carolina," she said.

"That's funny!" said Linda Lee (or was it Jeanette Ellen?). "That's your name, too."

"Yes," said Carolina. "All my brothers and sisters are named for places. We traveled quite a lot in my family. My father is an airline pilot."

"*My* father doesn't work," Sondra announced. "At least that's what Mother says."

"Sondra's father's in the movies," explained Jeanette Ellen (or was it Linda Lee?). "What airline does your father fly for?"

"Time to meet the others!" trilled Mrs. Crouch, and Carolina trudged over to the next circle.

By the time tea was served in tiny cups with flowers painted on them, Carolina had a headache. She'd told at least three different stories, even though she knew the girls would compare notes later. Maybe she could explain that her father had a top-secret government job in a foreign country. She *couldn't* tell the truth without risking his life!

She'd messed up. And it was just the beginning.

The days were long and dreary. Most of Heather's books were boring, all about girls doing dumb things and getting into trouble. She helped Stefan with the birds and went for walks with Crow, but she thought about Melanie always.

Each morning when she awoke, the first thing she did was count the days until Melanie's next phone call.

Stefan was not allowed to leave the grounds.

At night Carolina would take her sleeping bag from the back of Heather's closet and sneak out the door to sleep under the pine tree with Crow.

On Friday morning she opened her eyes and saw Mrs. Crouch's bony ankles. She squeezed her eyes shut, and when she opened them again the ankles were gone.

She hoped it was a dream.

That night she and Stefan played Monopoly. Stefan won. He always did. "The rich get richer." He chuckled, scooping his fake money off the board into his lap. Real money didn't mean a whole lot to Stefan, but that was probably because he never had to worry about it. "You can't buy the best things," he said once.

She asked him for a "for instance." She remembered too many times when she and Melanie had to count pennies just to buy a quart of milk.

"Well," he considered, "for instance, you can't make dolphins jump out of the water if they don't want to, no matter how much money you have. And you can't buy friends. At least not real ones. You can't buy a good sunrise. Nope, not a decent sunset either . . ." He went on and on. Finally he said, "And you can't buy wings, no matter how much money you have. At least not yet."

"Time for bed, children," said Mrs. Crouch at the stroke

of ten, and stood holding the door until they left the room.

"Carolina?"

Carolina turned. "Yes, ma'am?"

Mrs. Crouch stood in the doorway of the den, a worried look on her face. Then she seemed to make up her mind about something she'd been thinking long and hard about. "Nothing, my dear. Go on up to bed."

Carolina waited in Heather's bed until she was sure everyone was asleep and then got her sleeping bag from the closet. In the glow of Heather's Barbie night-light Carolina's shadow stretched toward the door. The shadow's hand and then her real hand reached for the doorknob and turned it, but the door wouldn't open. She turned the knob again and jiggled the door in case it was stuck. Her heart fell.

She was locked in.

She ran to the window and pushed it open, even though she knew she couldn't climb down two stories to where Crow waited. "Crow!" she called. "Crow!"

A half-moon filled the patio with soft white light. She called again, and the black bird hopped out from wherever he'd been hiding and looked up. In his beak was something she couldn't quite see. "Here!" she whispered, patting the windowsill. "Come up here!"

Crow cocked his head.

"Up here!"

But of course he couldn't fly. There was no way he could get to her or that she could get to him. She watched him scurry off with his latest find. It was probably something that nobody, not even another bird, would notice. A pebble, a piece of string. But to Crow, it was treasure.

Heather's room was full of treasure, things she collected and that she must have loved. Barbies and bears, miniature horses, rings with shiny stones. Things her mother now loved in Heather's memory. For a while Carolina had thought this room held everything a girl could ever want. She'd been caught up, like Crow, with things that shone the brightest. But these were not her things, and this was not her room.

What Carolina treasured most in her life would be out of place on Heather's shelves. They were silly things, some of them, and some weren't even her own. A red sun hat, gold-plated earrings, ninety-seven books with worn paper covers, a T-shirt with dolphins on it, a photograph of a teenage boy leaning against a truck, a fishing lure that Crow had dropped into her hand from the deck of the *Mary Louise*. Then there were the things you couldn't put on a shelf at all. Like the smell of Melanie's just-washed hair, the way she snorted sometimes when she laughed, and then laughed about that. There was an old yellow school bus that talked in the night.

She climbed onto the windowseat and watched the patio below. She would stay awake all night if she had to. If a wild cat came after Crow, she'd throw a shoe or a book at it. She'd scream and yell and wake up the whole house. She'd do whatever it took to keep Crow safe until morning.

Maybe Mrs. Crouch thought she was keeping Carolina safe by locking her in, by offering her a house, a "real" family. But she had told Carolina that she must make up her own mind. She knew somewhere inside that you couldn't keep a person like a treasure.

You couldn't keep a bird either, not for long.

The moon was a bright half circle. It shone in a sky empty except for itself, empty of stars. Carolina thought about how much her mother loved moonlight. The man in the moon, she once told Carolina, was the only man who'd never let her down.

# 16

No matter how hard she tried to keep her eyes open, Carolina had finally fallen fast asleep on Heather's windowseat. She awoke when the sun hit her eyes. Leaning forward on the windowsill, she scanned the grounds for Crow. Her heart thudded with dread.

The door was unlocked. Carolina didn't spend much time thinking about Mrs. Crouch locking the door and then coming back sometime in the night to unlock it. Instead, she ran for the kitchen and the back door as fast as her bare feet would take her.

Crow wasn't far from his pine tree. He had found something flat and dead with a long skinny tail and he was pulling it this way and that.

"Come on inside, Carolina," called Stefan from the door. "Lupe's making cinnamon toast." He wheeled out to her. "Did you sleep outside again?"

She almost told Stefan that his mother had locked her in, but for some reason changed her mind. "Uh-uh" is all she said.

"And Crow's just fine. He took good care of himself."

"Sure he did." Carolina held out her hand and Crow leaped on. "Of course he did. What did you think?"

"Well, what I think," Stefan said in his serious, thoughtful way, as if she really expected an answer, "is that it's pretty hard to know anything for sure about a bird, Carolina. I mean, you can't think like a bird. You can't know what Crow wants. You never will. Humans can't do that."

Carolina gave a hopeless shrug and sighed. She was always thinking about what was best for Crow, who couldn't, after all, tell her.

Crow ruffled his wings. He looked from Carolina to Stefan, Stefan to Carolina, as if he knew they were talking about him.

Stefan shook his head. "He should be gone already, Carolina. His tail feathers are all grown in."

"He's thinking about it," she said. "*You* don't know."

"You think because he's not in a cage that he's free," Stefan said in a quiet, very firm voice. "But he's not. He's never been free."

"What do you mean?" cried Carolina, lashing out at Stefan because her own feelings were hurt. "*You're* the one who keeps animals in cages. *You're* the one who didn't want to let Frank go. What do you know about freedom?"

As soon as the words were out, Carolina wanted to snatch them back. How could she have said such a thing to Stefan, her best friend? Stefan who never knew the freedom of running across an open field. But Stefan only shook his head, not exactly sadly, and began to speak as if he'd been thinking for a very long time what to say about this thing called freedom. He spoke about the world he knew best, the natural world. He talked about dolphins, the great acrobatic swimmers of the ocean, which would never fly. About eagles, which could fish but would never learn to swim. About cheetahs, which could outrun any living thing but were losing their habitats day after day because humans felt free to take their land. About people like him who couldn't walk but whose minds and hearts were free as they let them be. "There's no such thing as absolute total freedom, Carolina. We all have things we can't do, or won't do, or aren't allowed to do. That's what it means to grow up." He stopped then, embarrassed that he'd gone on so long. "But Crow, *Crow* belongs to an entire other world, and it's time to let him go there."

"I know. I know you're right. I'm sorry, Stefan, for what I said—"

"It's okay." He did a quick wheelie, one of his best. "I'm sorry for the lecture. But I've got to start practicing big speeches—"

"I know, for when you're famous."

"Yeah." He grinned, and they were back on even ground.

Carolina found herself thinking about all the times Melanie talked about freedom, about how important their freedom was. But they were never really free. The bus that let them live the life of Gypsies was really just a cage they would never escape, not as long as Melanie chose to live life the way she did. Red was free, probably free as a human could be. But Melanie wasn't. According to Stefan, it was time for Melanie to grow up.

Carolina was free to choose where she would do her own growing up. But she knew in her heart that she had already made her choice. "I've got to go home, Stefan."

"I guess I knew that," he said sadly.

"I'm sorry . . ."

"Nah, you don't have to be sorry. I know you miss your mom."

"She needs me."

"But what about Red?"

"You mean, if he's there."

"Yeah . . ."

She shrugged. "It doesn't matter. I mean, it matters, but there isn't anything I can do about it. She'll just go on chasing him around, I guess. Maybe someday she won't. Or they'll get married. I don't know . . . I just know that I belong with her and Trinity. Whatever happens."

Mrs. Crouch came into the kitchen wearing a white quilted bathrobe with black buttons that made her look like a snow lady. "Good morning, children! Ah, Lupe, you dear woman. The coffee's made." She poured herself a cup, inhaling it before she took a sip. Mr. Crouch came padding in, reading the morning newspaper.

"Stefan," said Mrs. Crouch to her son, "I forgot until your father just reminded me that the Fiesta parade is this afternoon. Carolina's never seen it."

"Great," said Stefan halfheartedly.

"The Fiesta parade, Stefan. I thought you loved it."

"I do, but . . ." He tore the center out of his cinnamon toast, pushed it into his mouth, and began glumly to chew it.

"What's the matter, then?"

Carolina stood up, holding on to the back of her chair so they wouldn't see that her hands were shaking. "Mrs. Crouch? Mr. Crouch?"

"Yes, Carolina?" they said in one voice. Mr. Crouch laid his newspaper down.

"I've made up my mind."

Mrs. Crouch's sad wet eyes got sadder and wetter. She set her coffee cup very carefully on the counter. "Oh dear, I know what you're going to say. I do." Tears sprang into her eyes. "Don't mind me. I cry so easily. You've decided to go home, then, is that it?"

"Yes."

"No wonder Stefan's in a funk. Well!" Mrs. Crouch smiled bravely. "We can still go to the parade, can't we?" She looked at each of them in turn. "Well, can't we?" Carolina realized then just how much she liked Stefan's mother. It wouldn't be as easy to leave as she'd thought.

"I'll search for my old sombrero," said Stefan.

"It's never too soon to start," cried Mr. Crouch, finger in the air.

"And Carolina can wear Heather's Fiesta dre—" Mrs. Crouch almost caught herself in time. "Carolina can wear whatever she wants to."

# 17

They had gone as far as the edge of the cliff, Carolina and Stefan, Crow riding Carolina's shoulder as always. She'd grown so used to him being there that she didn't always realize when he wasn't. She hoped it would always be that way.

"I wish you weren't leaving," Stefan said sadly, pushing his wheels through the crackling leaves. "But it's okay. I mean, I understand. I just wish you were staying here. I wish you were living in your bus across the field."

"So do I," said Carolina.

After the parade and a big Mexican dinner, Carolina asked Mrs. Crouch's permission to sleep outside for the last time next to Crow. Under the pine trees and stars, she talked to Crow a long time, trying to explain the sky, the tops of trees, and the birds that he could love. "Dream about flying, Crow," she urged. "Dream about wind under your wings."

Stefan was waiting in the morning when she opened her eyes. Along with a pair of faded, ripped-up jeans, he was wearing the T-shirt she had given him, the one with dolphins jumping through rainbows.

They crossed the brick patio, the ground that was strewn with dry spiny leaves and seedpods, and came at last to the edge of the cliff. Side by side, they looked out into the ocean below and the sky that went on forever.

In the distance a line of pelicans played follow the leader, stringing low over the horizon. There were tiny sailboats in the distance and surfers sitting out the swell, their feet dangling free in the deep blue water. The world was full of space, and wind to move you through it.

Crow was perched lightly on the back of Carolina's hand. In the sunlight his feathers shone purple and green, magenta and gold. He was a beautiful bird. He'd been her bird, but only for a time. Truly, he belonged to no one but the wind.

She brought him to eye level on her bent arm. "It's time to be a bird," she said, looking him straight in the eye.

Crow cocked his head.

"You know what I'm saying, don't you? Don't you, Crow?"

Crow's black eyes glittered.

"It's time," she said, blinking back tears.

Stefan sat very straight in his chair, his mouth in a grim line. "Do it, Carolina," he urged. "His family will find him."

"I love you, Crow," she whispered.

She took Crow into her hands. She could feel his heart beating, or else there were hearts in her hands that beat along with his. "Fly, Crow!" she whispered into his ear. Then she held her arms straight out and, biting her lip so hard she tasted blood, tossed him into the air. "Fly!"

Crow dropped below the level of the cliff, almost too fast for the eye to see. Then out came his wings, two beautiful many-colored wings, the wings of black angels. He dipped in a low arc over the pounding surf, then with great strong beats of his wings took the air.

Stefan cheered. He clapped his hands wildly. "Yea, Crow!" he cried.

Carolina dropped her arms, her empty hands, to her sides. She felt like laughing and crying both, and could do neither one. Crow wheeled in the air as if he'd been flying all his life, or dreaming of flying, and knew all the right moves. He seemed to be showing off. Then suddenly he veered left and sailed toward the cliff again. With a light bounce, he landed on her shoulder. Carolina turned her face and felt, for the space of three breaths, his soft feathers against her cheek. And then he was gone. With a single bob of his tail he leaped into the air and sailed away, off toward the soldier trees. Carolina and Stefan watched until he became a tiny black speck in the air and disappeared.

Two weeks later Carolina stood in front of the room and introduced herself to the other sixth-graders in her class. "My name is Carolina Lewis," she said in a strong, clear voice. "I live with my mother and baby sister, Trinity, on a yellow school bus with blue curtains and ninety-seven books. Once I had a pet crow. My best friend's name is Stefan."

Stefan wrote every week, sending the letters to the post office, where Carolina could get them after school. His family all missed her, he said, "but me most of all." He told her that the morning Carolina let Crow go his mother had watched from Stefan's bedroom window and that she'd said later, more than once, how very brave Carolina was.

"Then things began to change around here," he said. His mother was learning how to say yes. He could see it wasn't very easy for her, but she said it anyway, more and more. Stefan had gone into town twice all by himself, and down to the harbor to see the fishing boats. He thought he might be able to come for a visit in the spring if he started working on his mother right now. He couldn't wait to get on an airplane, he said. He couldn't wait to fly.

**Valerie Hobbs** is the author of two novels for older readers, *How Far Would You Have Gotten If I Hadn't Called You Back?* and *Get It While It's Hot. Or Not.* She is the most recent winner of the PEN/ Norma Klein Award.

Valerie Hobbs lives in Santa Barbara, California, where she teaches writing at the University of California.